The Story
So Far...

Sheldon Currie

The Story So Far...

Happy Birthday 1999
to Daddy with love
from Anne-Marie & Michael

Breton Books
Wreck Cove, Cape Breton Island
1997

Editor: Ronald Caplan

Production Assistance: Bonnie Thompson

Composition: Glenda Watt

He Said (Parenthetically), Sanabitur Anima Mea, The Lovers, Jesus Creep, The Path, The Glace Bay Miners' Museum, and Lauchie and Liza and Rory appeared first in *The Antigonish Review,* between 1970 and 1981. The Accident was in *Canadian Fiction Magazine* in 1984, and *Best Canadian Short Stories* in 1985. Dies Irae was in *Canadian Fiction Magazine* in 1989. On Parle Par Coeur won the Okanagan Short Story Award and was published in *Canadian Author and Bookman* in 1983.

THE CANADA COUNCIL | LE CONSEIL DES ARTS
FOR THE ARTS | DU CANADA
SINCE 1957 | DEPUIS 1957
We acknowledge the support of
the Canada Council for the Arts for our publishing program.

We gratefully acknowledge support from Cultural Affairs, Nova Scotia Department of Education and Culture.

Canadian Cataloguing in Publication Data

Currie, Sheldon.

    The story so far...

    ISBN 1-895415-21-7

I. Title.

PS8555.U7S76 1997   C813'.54   C97-950144-X

PR9199.3.C82S76 1997

PRINTED IN CANADA

Contents

Publisher's Note

"HUMAN BEINGS are all caricatures," Sheldon Currie wrote in an essay about author Flannery O'Connor. "None of us is matter perfectly animated by spirit, and insofar as we are not, we are awkward, wooden, stereotypic, rigid, graceless, mechanical, robotic, and of course, comical."

Currie could have been speaking of his own work. In light of that, I have had the privilege of selecting the stories in *The Story So Far....*

With Currie's recent fame, I want to keep more of his work available, stories written before and after "The Glace Bay Miners' Museum"—the pivotal short story that became his very popular novel *and* the award-winning movie, "Margaret's Museum."

Many readers will be brought to this book because they have seen the movie and read the novel. They may be aware that the original short story—"The Glace Bay Miners' Museum," included in this collection—has proved successful in other forms as well. To list them all: The short story was published in *The Antigonish Review*, 1976. It actually started with a song, "The Ballad of Charlie Dave," which Sheldon wrote in Alabama in 1964. Playwright Wendy Lill developed the short story into a CBC radio drama, also called "The Glace Bay Miners' Museum." Then, based on the original story, Gerry Wexler and Mort Rancen wrote the script for the movie "Margaret's Museum," for which Sheldon wrote as his additional contribution the manuscript that became *The Glace Bay Miners' Museum—The Novel.* Wendy Lill then used the novel as the basis for her 1996 offering, *The Glace Bay Miners' Museum—The Stage Play.*

And still the fundamental story held.

A GOOD PART of Sheldon Currie's struggle has been to create ordinary people doing the outrageous in a way that is as believable as the daily outrageous acts of people we live among and are—from a reconstructed man with his feet on backwards to Margaret's public shrine/museum to Yvette's determination to create love in "On Parle Par Coeur." It seems to me that Currie's earliest stories are tales of mechanical people—often painfully normal, even obvious characters—each crippled by the obvious—by fear, by their marriage and/or job, by religion—just cool every-day automatons. Just average people. They touch, but there's no real flesh on those bones.

Then Currie's characters begin to take on vulnerability through stories like "The Accident" and "The Path." With "The Glace Bay Miners' Museum" and beyond, we have the outrageous acts by flesh-and-blood people, people daring to live out the warm and terrifying details of love.

These stories are as bizarre as a world that includes religion that transforms the mundane into the holy and a coal industry that treats human life as so much dung. The ridicule and profound respect in Currie's use of Latin liturgy are no more arbitrary than the conditions of labour or a fall of rock that takes one person and not another—that has no regard for roles as father, provider or lover—as cold, distant and intimate as God.

Sheldon Currie is not through with us. What I've chosen here—11 stories—is a sub-total, an accounting for the record, for now. Told with good humour and compassion—for Currie, for us—this is the story so far.

Ronald Caplan
Wreck Cove
Nova Scotia

He Said (Parenthetically)

EXCEPT FOR HIS NOSTRILS George was not a large man; except for his ears not round. He was followed across the length of the hotel lobby by three young tall handsome women in bawdy stockings and large gaily coloured hats. They had been behind him for some time. Many people in the lobby stared because who wouldn't? George, unaware of the three ladies, who wore felt-soled shoes, thought people were looking at him and, slightly overcome by panic, he forefingered his belt buckle, and hurried, making the dining room in ten seconds less than was his wont.

Seated, he was alarmed when three chairs of his table for four were suddenly occupied by three women wearing white lipstick and ironical smiles with impunity. "Who are these?" he expostulated silently.

"My name is Marg Mowse," said the young lady across the table. "Next to you is my sister, Liza; next to me is her sister, Jon."

"Wonder what they see in me," he queried, silently.

"Nothing," Marg said.

"What do you want to eat?" said the waitress, out loud.

"Mendellson's Pea Soup," answered Marg, equally loud, "for everyone."

"That's all?" queried the waitress, rhetorically.

Marg did not answer. No one else answered.

When the soup came, the girls ate theirs with dispatch. And in stony silence they stared at George while he ate his more slowly with his spoon. It took him fourteen spoonfuls to complete the work. He put his spoon in the soup bowl with a slight clank and announced:

"I guess I'll go to my room."

All rose.

Upstairs, Marg preceded George, who was followed by Liza and Jon down the long carpeted hallway in ambiguous procession. When Marg arrived at Room 14 she turned abruptly, causing her followers to pull up short. She thrust forth her beringed right hand and opened the door. She stared at the forehead of a bewildered George.

"My room is 15."

"Get in there."

Inside, George was amazed to find himself. Marg went to the bathroom and returned with an aerosol can with which she sprayed the occupant in absentia of Room 15. The effect was immediate and something like this (and I quote from the can): The patient is wholly anesthetized, yet conscious, and pliable at the major joints. Marg dropped the can with its unused portion into the wastecan (with a clatter).

"Take off his clothing," Marg ordered, with quiet amusement.

George fainted, but remained pliable in his major joints.

Awake, George found himself prone. Looking straight up from where he lay on his back he saw himself full length in a mirror. He saw the three women at his feet; Marg was supervising Liza and Jon who appeared to be, and indeed were, preparing to do some work with what appeared to be, and in fact were, instruments.

"Shave," Marg said, with barely concealed contempt.

Barely concealed, George watched while Liza, working the right side, Jon, working the left, covered his legs to about three inches above the ankle with Gillette super-foaming lather. In due course they dehaired George's benumbed limbs deftly. While Liza and Jon disposed of their hot pans full of water, lather and hair, George noticed that at this point his feet and legs up to three inches above his ankles were clean and shiny.

Meanwhile Marg stood transfixed staring at the bed at a point midway between George's ankles. The two ladies returned pushing trays which they wheeled up to the operating table, one on either side, beside George's feet. From a jar on a table behind Marg each girl took a fist full of a gelatin-like substance and covered George's feet and legs to about three inches above the ankles. The three women then sat down on a bench along one wall while they smoked a cigarette each. Having finished their cigarettes, they removed their gaily coloured hats.

Having removed their gaily coloured hats, they returned to their posts. Liza and Jon removed the gelatin-like substance with paper towel, while Marg looked on, bemused, steeling herself to the smoke which by now was all but entirely dissipated.

"Epidermis," said Marg.

Competent hands pulled like a sock the skin from the foot and leg, after carefully cutting a circumference about three inches above the ankle, and carefully stretched same over a sock tree which was handy. Same was then placed on a tray.

"Corium," said Marg.

Fillets were removed in three-inch-wide bloody strips and carefully placed on a tray near same. Bone and cartilage revealed seemed, and, indeed were, in perfect condition.

"Nails," said Marg.

Nails were removed. George looked on with barely concealed fascination.

"Phalange I," said Marg.

Wiping a bead of sweat from her brow with a barely perceptible kleenex, Jon began work on the left foot with what appeared to be, and indeed, in part were, lobster tools, and after what appeared to be, and in fact was, a certain amount of time, removed George's great toe, and placed it on the tray in a receptacle which was marked L Phalange 1. Clearly the events of the afternoon were not entirely spontaneous. Liza followed suit on the right side.

George became bored sometime during Phalange IV and slipped off, although remaining pliable in his major joints; consequently he missed Phalange V as well as all of the metatarsals and tarsals.

George woke up in Saskatchewan. He was standing in the middle of a prairie. As far as the eye could see he saw an apple orchard. Being fond of apples, he decided to strike out for the apple orchard. After five minutes, having failed to progress even a fraction of an inch, he began to suspect something amiss. Upon looking down he couldn't help but notice that his feet were on backwards. All was revealed in a flash. His brain trying to go in one direction, his feet trying to go in another, George was reduced to a state of equilibrium, and he remained motionless, although conscious, and pliable in all the major joints.

Sanabitur
Anima Mea

NO ONE EXPECTED A NUN to come in the door with aplomb. Nobody expected anyone to come in because everybody was already there: the men with their Johnny Walkers and their Canadian Clubs and their Vat 19s placed on the kitchen table, the women with their brownies and their squares and their crabmeat sandwiches on the arborite counter top. None, although a few had been vague Catholics, had ever even known a nun, or seen one, probably; and had they thought about it, which, of course, they had not, they would have thought that nuns had been replaced by, as a matter of fact, themselves, or others like themselves: social workers, psychologists, teachers, nurses, unemployment insurance agents, doctors and other horror show ticket takers.

They were all in the kitchen with their first drinks, taking their first sips. Unaccountably, they had all arrived at the same time, and the kitchen was so big and so comfortable that they stayed a while to mill and chat and to try a little harmless flirting. Hardy, Gloria's husband, poured Linda a triple Scotch because, although she was "a quiet little thing normally," when she "had a few" she was "a barrel of fun." George slipped his hand under Gloria's wax paper and snitched one of her brownies; he had gotten the notion that seeing people stealing her brownies made her quiver and feel vague about her husband who always said every chance he got that he hated her goddam brownies. Each tried to be amused by what the others said. Each chuckled at what the others did. It was Friday night and they were having a party. They enjoyed having parties.

They were all getting quite warm and cosy what with the heat from their bodies and what with their drinks and what with their matches and their cigarettes; and they were asking each other how their days had gone and how much butter was and eggs were, when she came in. A small square suitcase in her hand. A regular nun. Not the new kind. The medieval type. A black habit from head to foot trimmed with white around the face, neck and wrists. With a small square case and a million aplomb, she walked into the kitchen, said hello to everybody collectively, very cheerfully, and walked through the kitchen, down the few steps to the living room/dining room, where the party was to occur. Where she stopped, no one knew, she was out of sight, and no one had followed her from the kitchen.

In the kitchen they lit more cigarettes and did not take things in their strides. Shocked, maybe, was not it. Surprised? Perhaps. Perplexed? Yes. Each looked at some object in the room, as if pretending he were alone; and each was silent, as if the first to speak would somehow be thought to be implicated in whatever was happening. Then Ronald,

7

the social worker, poured himself another drink and said, "Anyone else?" and everybody relaxed noticeably but said nothing. They shifted their positions a bit. Some looked at each other's shoulders. They acted as if they had just had a telegram announcing the death of someone's father and they were wondering if the rest of them should continue the party or go home.

Finally the hostess announced, almost inaudibly, that the host would have to go in and interview the lady and find out what's what. The doctor's husband, Gerald, encouraged this course of action and suggested that the lady be told there was a party about to happen and she could stay ("if that's all right with Betty") "if the rules of her order don't forbid it." The doctor supported her husband, saying that all in all it was a sound plan. Fred, the nurse, suggested that perhaps Wanda being a female psychologist, should go "in case something wasn't quite right." When they asked her to perform this duty Wanda said simply, "Don't be crazy. The host should go. It's his joke."

So the host went but he stayed not long at all; in fact, he went in, wheeled, and returned without a stop. He came back gesticulating. Mute. Went to his bottle. The guests were puzzled but happier now that they had someone to look at.

"What is it?"

"What's wrong?"

"Well!"

The host could only point, indicating that someone

should go and see, but nobody went. They waited until he recovered.

"Naked," he said when he recovered.

"Naked?" they said.

"Naked," he said. He didn't whisper, but his voice was not meant to carry very far. "Naked. In there, naked as a cat. Her clothing is on the rug in the middle of the room and she is sitting on the piano stool without a tack."

"A nun!" they said. A nun is in the living room naked as a cat. That cannot be. It's a mistake. It's a trick. It's a joke. Who can she be? What can she be doing? How did she come here? Why is she in the nude? What are we going to do?

What shall we do?

What can we do?

We have to do something.

Well then, what shall we do—have a party in the kitchen while she occupies the rest of the house?

"Hold it. Hold it. Hold it," Gloria said. "Look—let's face it, this is the most exciting party we've had in years and it hasn't even started. There is a woman in there in the nude. We have all seen nude women. A nun is only a woman in disguise. If she is a nun. And now she is without her disguise. Why are we embarrassed? Let us go in and query this person about the various aspects of her visit."

So in they went. Placed themselves like doilies on the furniture. And indeed they found the young woman unattired as their host had described, although not as furry as a cat; the host was not a student of metaphor.

Her hair was black and came down over her shoulders in front and back. She had hair also on her arms, especially on her forearms; not too much, but you could notice it and might want to run your fingers along to see what it felt like. Her breasts were young, but full—not at all what you would expect to see on a nun—and quite shakey. Her pubic hair was dyed purple. The legs were modestly crossed.

The problem of what to do with this unconventional female was not solved simply by entering the room; so Wanda said:

"Do you come here to make love?"

"Goodness gracious, no," she replied.

"Well, you've taken off all your clothes. You don't appear to be about to take a bath." A lot of people laughed. She smiled at them.

"Don't you like to screw?" Gloria asked, rather vehemently.

"Well, frankly," she replied, "I do, but I had to give it up when I joined. We give up the lot. That's the main thing."

"You belong to an order?"

"Yes, the Sister of Free Love."

"You encourage Free Love."

"Yes."

"But you don't do it yourself?"

"Oh, yes, we love. We don't screw, but we do love."

"Who?"

"Who?"

"Who do you love?"

"We love everybody."

Gloria, who had taken the precaution of filling a water glass full of Vat 19 before coming into the living room suddenly got up from her chair and went up to the nun. She stood, uncertain for a moment, holding her glass in her left hand, then her free hand crashed across the woman's face.

"Do you love me?" she asked, in a low voice, hardly moving her lips.

"Yes."

Crash. She slapped her again. "Do you love me?"

"Yes. But I'm afraid I've upset you."

"Gloria," someone said, "what are you doing? The woman is crazy but she means no harm. Sit down and enjoy her for Christ sake."

Gloria changed the glass to her right hand and with her left hand smashed her again on the ear, and although the poor nun still smiled, tears began to fall along her nose.

"No harm," Gloria said as she turned and addressed the other guests who were transformed suddenly into an audience. "No harm. What the hell is she doing here, then? Why did she dye her hair? What has she got in that case?"

Gloria left the room. Her husband got up and went over to the nun and sat in her lap, with one arm around her neck, the other in front, his hand supporting a breast.

"Why did you dye your hair?" he said. "What have you got in that case?"

Gloria returned and threw the glass of Vat 19 over both. Hardy went back to his chair, laughing sheepishly. The nun cried softly as if she suffered a secret pain. She had the innocent look of a fresh wound. Droplets of Vat 19 glistened on her body, uncomfortable, beautiful.

A sympathetic voice came from somewhere in the room. "Perhaps you could tell us why you came?"

"Yes," she said softly. "I came to help anyone who might want to give up smoking."

"You are crazy," someone said, not sympathetic.

"That's why I came," she said.

"Is that what nuns do? Isn't there something important for nuns to do, like what about serving in hospitals in jungles?"

"I'm only a novice," the nun replied. "I'm not allowed to do anything until I learn; till I get experience. You can see what a botch I'm making. But it's not important—you know, you have to start somewhere."

"Start what?"

"Giving up."

"For what?"

"For love."

"You give up smoking for love?"

"You give up everything."

"You give up screwing for love?"

"Yes."

"Isn't that self-defeating?"

"Well, I'm not sure how it works. I was told and I be-

12

lieve it but it's hard to remember. Like, love is free, you know. You give yourself for nothing, not for fun or anything. I don't know. I knew, but I can't explain. I'm just a crazy nun."

"That does make sense," someone said.

The nun got up and turned out the lights and opened her suitcase and flipped a switch, and on the wall appeared a picture of a huge room full of people.

"This is a doctors' convention," the nun said. "There are three hundred people in that room. Only four people are smoking. Why? Because doctors realize what smoking can do."

"This next slide," (she flicked a switch) "shows what smoking can do." The picture showed a man with tubes sticking up his nose. He was pushing a cart and the tubes came from a container on the cart. "This man can not take in oxygen in the regular fashion," she said, "and he gets it from the container. He has to push the container wherever he goes."

Everybody moved to the kitchen except Rodney who didn't smoke but the nun showed all her slides anyway, and commented on them. When it was over Rodney asked her if she wouldn't like to go to his apartment and show them again, but she said no that she gave that up for good. "Otherwise," she said, "I'd love to."

She put on her clothes and went to the kitchen and spent a little time in small talk before departing.

"How many are there in your order, Sister?"

"There's only one of us so far," she said. "But we're growing, I hope."

"Good night."

"Good night."

The Lovers

HIS LOVE WAS STILL ALIVE. Often enough George was surprised to discover a refinement of a depth in Thelma, and the eternity he had seen in her in their first year never became a mere memory. Their ten years were filled with routine, and more often than not, dull breakfasts, vacations, birthdays, visits, parties, friends, T.V. and intercourse, but now and then ignited by seconds, days and even weeks of sometimes soft and sometimes exciting delight in each other, in their children, in everything, and in nothing. Yet in their tenth year George grew tired of his wife, or his life, and he fell into depression. And during the year a crisis developed out of his general disposition and two coincident events: on the same day, his mother-in-law broke her leg playing hockey and his secretary fell down a flight of stairs in her apartment house and died after a series of heart attacks on the way to hospital.

On the way to the train George Jr. and Jake in the back seat cried in discord.

"George," Thelma said. "Be calm. For God's sake. You're all excited. You're perfectly capable of being alone for a week or so."

"You said three weeks."

"O.K. Three weeks. For three weeks. You can come up on the weekends; leave early Friday, come back early Monday morning. That leaves Tuesday, Wednesday and Thursday. Three days. Anyway, George, I've been nagging you to death for two months. You'll have some privacy. You said it. You said it yourself. Leave me alone, Thelma, for God's sake leave me alone.... The milk. Don't forget to leave a note to cut down the milk.... My God. It's not my fault my mother broke her leg. It's not her fault."

"Why does a woman nearly fifty years old want to play hockey? Checkers. For Christ sake, what's wrong with checkers?"

"You know damn well, George, that mother is an active woman. She's all alone."

"She should have a nurse."

"She can't afford a nurse."

"We'll pay."

"She hates nurses."

"There's the train."

"Kiss the kids."

"Bye, Daddy."

"Bye, George."

"Bye, Daddy."

"Bye, Jake."

"George, you'll be up on the weekend?"

"Yes."

"Yes. I love you."

"I love you too."

"What about your secretary?"

"The funeral's Sunday. It'll be very sad. She has no family left. Unless you count me. I'll have to take care of everything."

"I mean what will you do for a secretary next week?"

"Temporary help."

"I really wish I could be there."

"I know. It'll work out."

"Bye. I love you."

"Good bye."

"Bye."

"Bye."

The train went. George went home.

MONDAY MORNING George's temporary secretary appeared on her 21st birthday, all flags flying, with a simple greeting: "I'm from the sec's pool." Such a breast and bum he had never before seen, and blond long hair scattered over her shoulders, cherubic face and eyes and figure and sweater and skirt. A beautiful dunderhead, he thought. But no, not at all: efficient, writing letters, tic, tac, tic, without an error, without a smudge, two magnificent knees sticking out from the side of the desk, casual, flawless, sitting erect, everything done with her eyes on the opposite wall as if watching a foreign film with sub-titles.

Tuesday, he simply made notes, and passed them to her. She wrote the letters, he signed them, she folded, enveloped, licked, sealed, licked, stamped—they were gone. Law

terms were no problem. She knew enough. About everything else she knew more than he did. She corrected mis-
spellings, sharpened punctuation. By noon the work was
done. He took the afternoon off to complete post-funeral
arrangements; she re-arranged his files and chucked out
useless garbage.

Wednesday. He arrived to find three piles on his desk:
the biggest pile identified as "not worth your notice, answers to these letters are typed, ready for your approval."
He carefully examined the answers, signed each one and
passed them to her for folding, enveloping, stamping and
sending. He moved to pile three, identified as "worth your
notice," two letters from his wife. He read them: his mother-in-law's cast, Jake's sniffles, George's new shoes, love and
p.s., a note to the milkman to cut down the milk. Gabriele
went off to mail the letters. With the three paper hills gone,
his desk was finished. He looked ahead to lunch and a va-
cant afternoon. She has almost worked herself out of a job,
he thought. What a creature. Gorgeous. A sword came from
nowhere, entered the space between the two ribs closest to
his heart, and pierced gently the balloon of his depression.
Life is dull, routine, boring, sated, but seldom does a year
go by but some miraculous finger tickles a rib.

Wednesday afternoon, lunch in bellies of boss and secretary: sitting behind desks with nothing to do. No problem
for her. She wrote fifteen letters; she seemed to have lots of
friends. She went twice to the washroom; the door snapped
shut...silence...water, flushing...water running, the door

snapped open; the operation seemed to him somehow incongruous.

"Miss Smith."

"Yes."

"You don't talk much."

"I don't mind talking though.... Until now I've been quite busy. And you're not in the mood for talking. Depressed. It's very sad about your secretary. She was with you a long time. You must be very sad."

"Yes. I am very sad. But I've been thinking about you. You are a rather phenomenal secretary. Surprising."

"Surprising?"

"Yes, I would say surprising."

"Why?"

"Well. To be frank. When a girl shows up—beautiful, one does not expect efficiency too. Prejudice, I suppose."

"I've been well-trained."

"Obviously."

"Is it so obvious?"

"No, it's just obvious. You do a good job. You don't make mistakes. You don't see that often. It cheers a person up."

"I'm glad to hear you say that. You've had a bad experience.... Your secretary dying. You need cheering up. You've been quite depressed, haven't you? You were quite attached...fond of your secretary."

"I knew her for quite a long time. She made a lot of mistakes. A very sad affair, the funeral. Me and a hired priest and a corpse. Very sad. Very sad. But her death does not depress me."

"But you are depressed."

"Yes. I am depressed. Not by her death. I am depressed because she made many mistakes. And I was fond of her. I don't mind her dying. We are both better off. I don't suppose you understand that."

"I understand perfectly."

"You're too young to understand perfectly."

"I've never experienced depression. But I've met others."

"I can understand that. Unrequited love, I suppose."

"No, that's not it. No. Depression doesn't come from others."

"I don't suppose it does. No." He thought of his wife and their fatigued breakfast table, their tired bed, their kids who until recently carried them through troughs from peak to peak, and he recalled the earlier exciting breakfasts and beds. He remembered a toboggan ride with the kids. How excited they became. They meant to buy a toboggan the next week. Instead they paid fifteen dollars for a set of books on sex. He remembered how much they learned about graphs and statistics.

"Mr. MacMillan."

"Yes."

"Do you enjoy intercourse?"

"I'm not much of a socialite," he replied. "I go to the odd party."

"I mean sexual intercourse."

"What a strange question for a secretary to ask her employer."

"Does it matter if it's strange, if it's the right question?"

"Right for what?"

"Right for your state of mind."

"Are you reading my mind?"

"Yes."

"I'm amazed," he said, "that such a young pretty thing would be brazen enough to ask such a question."

"I am young. I am brazen. You name a thing, you find out if you're scared of it. Name it, and if it's really scary you're still scared. If a tidal wave is coming and you say tidal wave you're still scared. If you're scared to say shit, but say it, nothing happens."

George could not find a suitable reply.

"Just now," she said, "I asked you if you liked intercourse, and you avoided answering by replying as if you misunderstood. But you understood perfectly. See how easy it is to read your mind. I asked the question that way out of deference to your age. I didn't want to shock you too much. What I meant to ask was quite ambiguous. Do you like to screw, Mr. MacMillan?"

"Are you trying to take me for a toboggan ride?"

"Why not? You're depressed. I'd like to fix you up."

"Well.... What's your next move?"

"Are you really interested?"

"Is your method guaranteed?"

"Unconditionally but not absolutely."

"You sound like a lawyer."

"God forbid," she said.

"Is it a permanent cure?" he said.

"Nothing is permanent. Some things are continuous. It might be continuous. Depends on you."

"That's the trouble. Nothing is guaranteed. Nothing absolute. Nothing permanent. Everything usually depends on oneself."

"You're getting philosophical, Mr. MacMillan, and philosophy, sooner or later, leads to bullshit. I'm not much good at that. What you say is true, of course. But everyone needs a bit of help now and again."

"And you are going to help me?"

"Yes."

"Go ahead."

"O.K. First of all, I'll talk a bit."

"A sermon?"

"I doubt if you'll think it a sermon, Mr. MacMillan."

"O.K. Go ahead."

"You're thirty-five years old. You've been sitting there surreptitiously watching my breasts and knees. When I go to the toilet you watch my ass. It excited you. That's understandable...inevitable. I have young breasts, young knees, young ass. I like them myself. I dress sexy, and you are like most men who love their wives. Are you cured yet?"

"No, but it's getting better."

"You will be cured though. But this is not a hospital."

"You're finished talking then."

"Oh. Yes. Talking's nothing."

"What will you do?"

"Tomorrow's Thursday. All my work is done. Let it pile up tomorrow."

"You're going to take the day off?"

"Yes. If you don't mind."

"Will that fix my depression?"

"Not by itself. But tomorrow you will come to my apartment for supper. About six."

"I don't know if I like this cure. Instead of feeling depressed I'll feel guilty. After a while I'll be both depressed and guilty."

"Don't jump to conclusions, Mr. MacMillan."

"I'll try not to. Tell you the truth, I'm beginning to feel a bit silly."

"Of course. But that's because you still have conventional ideas. You're getting to the conventional age, you know, Mr. MacMillan."

"If I'm going to have supper with you, would you mind not calling me Mr. MacMillan."

"Yes, that's rather conventional too. But I don't care. It's immaterial to me. So long, Fido. See you tomorrow."

Tomorrow turned out to be a long day. He tried to think. This is not real, he thought: A young girl comes here, young, beautiful, vivacious, and instead of doing her work and going home to try to decide which of her young suitors to accept, she decides to seduce me, a married man with two children, a lawyer not terribly successful, almost twice her age. I'm not even a father image, he thought. She talks to me as a peer. The idea appealed to him, but he couldn't quite believe it. I don't believe it, he thought. It's not real. But he did believe it. Yet, because he did not altogether believe it, he never quite decided not to go. And when the time came, because he had not decided not to go, he went, up seven flights to her apartment, and with just enough alcohol in his brain to convince himself that this night's activity was nothing more than the psychological equivalent of a toboggan ride. His slight knuckle tap seemed to open the door, and with her hand on the knob stood Gabriele smiling.

"Hi," she said. "Come in."

"Thank you," he said, and followed her to the middle of the room. They seemed to be in a three-room apartment. Opposite the entry were two windows. In each wall to the left and right opposite each other was a door leading to another room. The floor was hardwood, covered with varnish. The windows were uncovered, the walls were painted green. There was one moveable object, a pole lamp with three sockets and shades, each with a blue bulb. There was no overhead fixture; the lamp lighted the room.

"Sit down," said Gabriele, "if you don't mind sitting on the floor."

George sat down on the floor. Gabriele sat gracefully down in front of him.

"Would you like to talk?" she asked. "I thought we

could sit here a while and relax. We can talk though if you like, if you think of anything you really want to say. Let's just sit here and look at each other."

George felt embarrassed but he did as she bid him.

She wore a bit more eye shadow, more subdued lipstick than in the office. Her blond hair fell in the same way over her shoulders. It was held from her face by two butterflies at the temples. She wore a sleeveless smock of golden silk, buttoned down the middle, falling short of her hip-hung slacks so that four inches of flesh were exposed, two inches below and two inches above her belly button. Her toenails were painted green.

At the beginning of her sitting session George observed Gabriele obliquely, but after ten minutes he relaxed a bit and then he simply looked at her while she looked at him. He was surprised to discover that they could find a middle ground between staring at each other and avoiding each other's eyes. After fifteen minutes, however, he began to suspect that something was expected of him. Otherwise he had lost his sense of awkwardness, but he was becoming physically uncomfortable. He had been sitting with his weight mostly on one hip with his legs curled to the side and behind him and with his right hand on the floor supporting the weight of his upper body. He decided he would have to do something. The idea came to him that she expected him to touch her. It occured to him that he didn't really want to touch her, for he half-felt himself in a trance which he did not want to break. Reluctantly he straightened up and felt pleasure at the release of the physical tension his body had been suffering. He leaned forward and stretched his arm and with his forefinger touched her belly button. She reacted by taking a deep breath, pushing her belly against his finger, then she said:

"Don't do that, George, you'll spoil everything."

Bewildered again, but relieved, George withdrew.

"Make yourself more comfortable," Gabriele said gently, and she showed him how, sitting erect with her right leg outstretched, the left foot resting on the right thigh. He complied. For comfort he let his foot rest on his knee rather than his thigh. She took his shoes and stockings off and tickled each foot a second. She sat back and they sat silent again. It's up to her then, he thought: God only knows what's going on.

After fifteen minutes she asked, "Feel good?"

"Yes," he answered. "Pretty good."

"Do you feel bewildered?"

"Yes, I do. But it doesn't matter as much to me as it did when I first came, which seems a long time ago."

"Did you go to the office today?"

"Yes."

"Did you work?"

"No. I sat there."

"Thinking?"

"No. Feeling guilty. Knowing that I might betray my wife if I had the chance."

"I know what you mean. But that was unnecessary.

You'll do no harm to your wife."

"Perhaps to myself, or my marriage."

"That's always a possibility. Although it's never necessary."

"I don't know what you're talking about," he said gently.

"I know you don't," she said gently.

"What did you do all day?" he asked.

"I got ready for tonight."

"Did you take the whole day off?"

"No, but I had to clean up the apartment, that didn't take long, and I had to prepare the food. And like you, I had a good few hours to prepare myself. And, oh yes, I had to get dressed. I did that last. Just before you came."

"How long did that take?"

"Fifteen seconds."

"Fifteen seconds?"

"Yes. I took off my brassiere."

Disconcerted, George said quickly, "You were already dressed then."

"Yes. I dressed this morning when I got up."

"Why do you have no furniture?"

"I don't need any," she answered abruptly and George felt rebuked. So he said quickly, "What did you fix for supper?"

"I broke some cheese."

"Cheese?"

"Yes. Cheese. Don't you like cheese?"

"Oh yes. I like cheese very much."

"I'm glad. I hate to make a mistake with this kind of thing."

"What kind of thing?"

"I also poured the wine. So that's ready. I don't have a knife. I thought we could just break the bread with our fingers. That O.K.?"

"Oh yes. That's fine."

They fell silent. They stayed silent for twenty minutes. George began to feel quite unreal.

Finally Gabriele spoke. "What are you thinking?" she asked.

"I wasn't. I was just feeling the floor with my behind."

"Your ass, you mean."

"Yes, my ass."

She said, "I thought perhaps you were thinking about your wife. Feeling guilty."

"My wife seems very remote."

"Would she be jealous if she knew you were here?"

"Oh yes. Indeed she would. She's quite jealous. Not only of women. Of anything."

"Do you like painting?"

"Yes."

"Do you have a favourite?"

"Yes. *The Lovers* by Picasso."

"It's quite classical."

"Yes."

"Is that why you like me?" she said.

"What do you mean?"

"I'm classical. I have a classical nose."

"Well, anyway, my wife would be jealous."

"Of the painting?"

"Of you."

"Do you love *The Lovers*?"

"Yes, you might say that."

"If you spent every Sunday looking at it, would she mind?"

"Yes. She'd feel left out."

They fell silent for a few moments.

He said, "Is this a three-room apartment?"

"Yes, it is," she answered. "This is the sitting room. The kitchen and bathroom are through that door behind you. And through the door behind me is the game room. I think we've had enough chit-chat. Let's go to the kitchen. We're getting boring."

They got up and went to the kitchen. There was nothing in it but a non-operating refrigerator and built-in cupboards; not a sign of a moveable object except two large wine glasses full of wine, a plate full of broken cheese and a loaf of French bread.

"Did you have anything to drink before you came?" she asked.

"Yes."

"O.K. You better have a leak now so we won't be disturbed. Come into the game room when you're finished."

For some reason or other, George smiled.

"One more thing," she said. "You look a bit silly in that business suit. Why not take off the coat and tie?"

"O.K.," he said, and went to the toilet.

Three minutes later he opened the door to the game room in pants and shirt sleeves. She was sitting on a green carpet in the middle of the floor. There was no furniture in the room. She beckoned and he sat in front of her as in the sitting room, but with legs crossed Buddha fashion, following her example. Between them on the floor was a deck of cards and a cribbage board. To the side she had placed the cheese, the wine and the loaf of bread.

"Do you play crib?" she asked.

"Yes."

"Good—let's play."

They played for fifteen minutes until she suddenly stopped in the middle of counting her hand. She looked at him quizzically. "Do you like my breasts?"

"Yes."

"Beautiful, aren't they?"

"Yes."

"You've never seen them though?"

"Not in the flesh."

"Do you know why I took off my brassiere?"

"No," George answered. He was beginning to feel real again. "Why did you take it off?" he managed to say. For a moment he thought he would lose his voice.

"Because it's very awkward for a man to take off a woman's brassiere. And even if he slips it off unobtrusively, the thing looks grotesque lying around on the floor. It doesn't look like one but it reminds me of a coffin. Actually I don't need to wear one anyway, but I wear one to keep my nipples from showing through my blouse. I don't want to be provocative on the street." By the time she had finished her little speech, he was excited.

"Let's play some more," she suggested, and they played for ten minutes. Then she opened the buttons down her blouse and folded one panel back under her arm. "Look at that," she said.

"I am looking."

"Does that make you horny?"

"Yes."

"Good. Let's play some more." They played. Then she stopped again. "Reach over and hold it in your hand," she said. He did.

"It's beautiful, isn't it?"

"Yes, it is," he replied.

"What would you think would happen if someone came along with a knife and chopped it off?"

For some reason or other, unperturbed, George found the perfect answer.

"It would bleed."

"Then what would happen?"

"You'd have to have it fixed."

"But if it were chopped altogether off."

"Then that would be the end of it."

"What if someone chopped *The Lovers* in pieces?"

"That would be the end of *The Lovers*."

"But there's a difference."

"What difference?"

"Blood."

"Oh. I see. I think I see. Actually I'm quite confused but I see a bit." He let go her breast and they played some more. After ten minutes he confessed, "I'm bored playing cards."

"Are you?" she said. "I like cards. The rules are absolute. You never have to guess if you know the rules. And the rules are all in a book."

He said, "I thought you said you weren't a philosopher."

"I'm not. I was just saying I like to play cards."

"If you're not a philosopher, what are you?"

"I'm a girl."

"What kind of girl?"

"A classical girl. A very good secretary."

"I should say you are."

"If you don't want to play, let's eat. I'm starved."

"O.K."

"Want to wash your hands?"

"No."

"Good. Pass me a piece of cheese." They each broke off a piece of bread and a piece of cheese and drank some wine. Then Gabriele took off her blouse. George became excited.

"Are you horny yet?"

"Yes."

"O.K. See how long it lasts."

It lasted ten minutes.

"It's over," he said.

"Why are you smiling?" she asked.

"Oh, I was just thinking. This is not real, is it?"

"Oh yes," she said. "Everything's real."

"This isn't."

"You felt me, didn't you?"

"Yes. But you don't feel quite real."

She stood up and took off her slacks.

"Feel my ass," she said. He did. "Is it real?"

"Yes. It's real," he said, becoming aroused.

"Make love to me," she said pulling him up. "See if it's real."

They began pressing and kissing until George began to lose control.

"Excuse me," she said. "I have to go to the toilet," and she walked naked through the door.

When she came back he said, "I've been thinking about my wife."

"I thought you would be," she said. "I didn't really have to go. But I thought I should."

"You're really quite beautiful."

"Yes, I know. But you think you'd better go."

"Yes."

"I'll put my clothes on."

"Good idea."

"You don't want to make love to me, as they say?"

"Well," he said, "I would like it, if you just think of it by itself. But all in all it wouldn't work, would it? It'd be like *The Lovers* were really lovers. That'd be the end of *The Lovers*."

"You were supposed to be knocked out of your depression," she laughed.

"I am. It's sad though."

"What is?"

"Dying."

"Let's go," she said. They put their clothes on, put the leftovers in a bag she took from her purse. She opened the hall door and with the light shining in, took the pole-lamp apart in three sections, and out she went, George behind her, down the stairs, refused a drive from George and took a taxi.

Jesus Creep

MINNIE WOKE UPSET and sat up on the edge of the bed. Because the bed was high, or her legs not long enough, her feet dangled short of the floor three inches. Her hands rested beside her on the sheet. Her attention focused on a worm which had invaded her lower intestine and was at the moment tooling around, looking for something to eat, an activity it pursued in the early hours after midnight. After studying its movements for some consecutive nights, Minnie concluded that it was about four and a half inches long and multilegged. She imagined that the end of its long range plan was to get to her stomach where there was a bowl of undigested alphabet soup.

Minnie always drank/ate a bowl of alphabet soup before she went to bed because she loved to lie in bed while waiting for the worm and think of her stomach as a poorly constructed typewriter trying to arrange itself to accord with the conventional keyboard. The fact that there were no numbers in the brand of soup she consumed bothered her not at all, because she knew that numbers could always be written out one, two, three, just as broken bits of letters would serve for all the punctuation marks she'd ever have use for. Minnie was semi-literate, but she had a metaphorical cast of mind and while her belly growled she would think of lines like:

A Blank Wall

Is no Bed of Roses

But why should it Be

and she'd say quietly to herself—"Now if I could write good enough I'd put that down and work on it."

She heard her sister Annie in the next room thrashing around in her bed-clothes and she turned slightly and said to what she referred to as her "great hulk of a husband": "Annie has led not the usual type of life which is why she stirs in her sleep." She expected and received no reply because, besides being deaf, her husband was asleep, but she continued to look at the heap of blankets as she quietly continued her barely audible speech.

"Annie didn't know nothin' about her past till she was four. Didn't even think about it till one day Mother gave her her first soft-boiled egg and said: 'The marriage was falling to shreddies, so Celia said I'll get you a baby to adopt 'cause it's well known that babies save marriages that are falling to bits, often in the nick of time. Celia was the welfare officer part time and she got you and gave me you, and here you are makin' the marriage worse if that's possible. Where Celia got you I don't know, she never did tell me.'

"Annie seemed pleased with this answer, or with her soft-boiled egg," Minnie would have said/written had she been literate and steeped in the modern tradition. "Annie, when she had swallowed the most of it, inquired further:

36

'And where did my mother, whomever she was, get me?'

"'Well, now, that,' she said, 'I could not relate. The fuckin' stork, no doubt.'

"Neither Annie nor Mother knew that I was right by when this talk was takin' place though I didn't hear it, of course, 'cause foetuses don't have ears; 'fact, Mother had gone to Celia and told her the baby didn't work, the marriage was still falling, thirty-two feet per second per second, and Celia said, 'Perhaps you need another dose' and she promised to do her best, and she was doing her level best every chance she got till Mother called and told her cease and desist that she had quite a little surprise for her. Celia seemed pleased but said she wisht she had let her know a little sooner.

"So I came upon the scene. And my father said, 'Oh, for Christ's sake, one wasn't bad enough?'

"But up we grew, unwelcome as we were. And we became fast friends, running through the hay, eventually boarding the school bus to commence erudition.

"Of course, it turned out Annie was the smart one," Minnie said to the heap of blankets, "slipping through the standard curriculum like a snake through a barrel of pus, outside of which she took enrichment in music and art and making belts and wallets, while I lagged. I lagged like a crippled rabbit, sometimes on three legs, sometimes on two. I lagged at fractions, and lagged at percentage and lit and chem and even phys ed. I couldn't even skip right. Till at last the piper got fed up from not being paid and I had to stay home and sweep the floors, while Annie was given every chance. So in the evenings division of labour was the thing and I stayed in the kitchen washing dishes and such, only half literate, while Annie went upstairs and yelled magazines at our deaf father.

"At last college came and took her away, while I lagged behind and seemed to be married to my father and mother. She stayed till the spring, working her way through by playing the piano in a night club and meeting all sorts of fruit-cakes so when she came back you couldn't understand a word she said on the telephone to her friends, although in the house she talked half literate English like me, but not often, and she yelled it like she was talking to our father who went upstairs.

"It was lonely. I was lonely before she came home, but after she came home I was lonelier because I figured I wouldn't be lonely once she got home. Then when she went away again it was even worse. So I went down the road next door where you were, you hulk, a man deaf like my father, and like my father most of the time asleep. I should've known better but instead I managed to slip under you when you were half asleep or half awake, and slip you in, and the next thing I'm married to you instead of my father and mother, but could hardly tell the difference.

"And so.... And so. You moved in. Sold your farm: a house, a barn with no roof, and a row of cracked radishes, and moved in with me and my forebears, and so they died right off and who could blame them? Meantime Annie was gone and not a word in the mail. Till February, a knock came on the door and who is there but herself in the freezing cold, not a goddam stitch on her back or front.

"'Let me in,' she said, 'I'm crazy.' Right down there at the very back door we still got right now. So in she came. Took off all her clothes at the bottom of the driveway and poked her naked legs into three foot snow, all the way up to the door and knocked. Had a cup of tea and said: 'I got to start again. I only want to stay till breakfast,' she said as she went to bed, and who could say her nay outside yourself who only could say, 'Who needs a nut creeping around the house even if she's naked?' Stunned as a bag of clawhammers.

"'I'm off,' she said after breakfast. 'Off. Off. Off.'

"'Where?'

"'Trade School.'

"'For?'

"'Electricity.'

"'Why?'

"'It's useful. You can get a job. You can go around and fix things for people. You make them happy, and they're glad you came and did it. There's not much you can do without electricity, people are so used to it.'

"She was quite young in those day. Who wasn't?

"Anyway you didn't give her a good word to go with, but she got away without it; an old dress from the attic she wore in High School, and carrying a brown paper bag full of underwear. No money. She said she had her resources.

"Never heard of her again till three years later I got a letter. I'll read it to you, since you can't hear," Minnie said. Her husband turned over in his sleep, woke up, astonished, maybe, to see his wife, sitting on the edge of the bed, turned toward him moving her mouth, holding her hand in front of her, as if she were reading.

Dear Minnie,

I did the whole thing. I can fix anything that has electrons flowing. Stayed three years and finished. At the end I met this guy with short hair and dirty fingernails. A plumber. So we said we'd live together and he'd do the plumbing and I'd do my electricity and be happy. So we did. We got married. Lasted twenty-four hours. Next day I came home and he was there drinking beer. So I sat down with a beer. And he said: "Get out in that kitchen and rattle them pots and pans." And I said; "What's a pan; and for that matter, what's a pot?" That very night he beat the piss out of me. So fuck that route. Now I bought myself a kind of hut near a nearby river. It's very comfortable, but, funny thing is, only thing I have not got is electricity. No poles around to take it from. I hire out to wire houses and get a job in construction when they can't get nobody else. It's very nice. Very sad but very nice. Hope you are getting along.

Annie

"And that was the letter," Minnie said to her husband, who had refallen asleep, and Annie, in the next room, stirred.

"And that was the last I hear, till years and years, a knock came and who was there but herself in the same old dress, and for all I know the same paper bag, and who knows maybe the same underwear, and said: 'And here I am again a small frail girl and old, and nearly naked.' And there she is in the next room, stirring in her sleep."

Minnie pushed herself off the bed and stood. She was disturbed by the noise in the cellar and didn't want to get closer to it, but knew she wouldn't get to sleep without her ritual cup of tea. And she knew that once she started down, Annie would come to help—every night she came to help. "What you need is not tea," she would say, "but to take your scissors and plunge them into that heap of guts on your bed."

And down Minnie went and Annie padding behind her. "And how many cups of tea have you had in the last god knows how many years and what good did they do?"

Minnie drank her tea in silence. Annie tapped a spoon on the sugar dish. Minnie drank her dregs and came to a difficult decision. "We must investigate the cellar."

"Yes," Annie said. "There is certainly something going on in the cellar."

"Music."

"Yes, there is certainly music."

"Clanks."

"Yes, there is often a definite clank."

"Clinks."

"Yes, I have often heard the clinks myself."

"Laughter."

"I have heard several laughs."

"Sobs."

"And sometimes sobs. And one side of a triangular conversation."

"One of us must go," said Minnie, "but I'm scared."

"I am sore afraid myself. I cannot go," Annie said, "for as you well know, I am an electrician, not a private investigator; therefore, you yourself must go whilst I prepare you a second cup of tea."

"Are you certain?"

"Well, what if the kettle should break down? Could you fix it?"

"No."

"Well there you have it. Put your sandals on in case you step on something squishy."

WHEN SHE HAD FINISHED her second cup of tea, Minnie said: "What we have in our cellar is quite the thing. We have a hole in the floor six feet long and three feet wide and deep, deep. The dirt is piled up on one side. On the other side we have a table and sitting at the table we have Cassie."

"Cassie?"

"Yes, Cassie. Celia's girl."

"What is she doing?"

"I asked her that. Said she plays solitaire, listens to country and western, and drinks beer, and waits."

"What is she waiting for?"

"I asked her that. Said she's waiting for events to run their course."

"Did you ask her up?"

"Yes. I asked her that. Said she would not put a foot to stair till events ran their course."

"I see. Well, let's go back to bed."

"I think perhaps I might better have a cup of tea."

"You had two cups of tea."

"Yes, but I think I can't sleep with the noise. Bad enough when I didn't know what it was."

"We'll turn off the light in the cellar."

"What good?"

"There will be no noise made in the dark. You'd be surprised how many things you can't do without a wire."

"Yes, but there is a switch down there."

"Yes, but turn it out anyway. May take her a while to find the switch in the dark and you'll be asleep by then. To-morrow I'll fix a switch in your room so you can turn off the cellar lights without getting out of bed."

And so it came to pass. The next night Minnie lay on her back tracing her worm through her guts when the bare-ly audible strains of the Tennessee Waltz first reached her ears. Her fingers fumbled on the floor beside her bed and flicked the switch Annie had installed for her convenience and went to sleep almost immediately. The faint smell of burnt flesh touched her nose only when it was too late to wake and so there was the whole night for her blood to car-ry the message, to familiarize every nook and cranny of her body with the brutal facts, so that when the message was delivered to her mind in the morning just before she woke up she was already used to it. The conversation in the hall was predictable: "I am an electrician not a mortician and Minnie is not strong, she is weak, she is also meek, but you have inherited the earth. Why did you bring that shovel up here? There is certainly nothing up here to shovel...."

The Accident

HE COULD STILL REMEMBER the hand he had when the phone rang. The seven, three, queen and five of spades, and the three of hearts turned up. Fifteen-two, fifteen-four, fifteen six and pair of threes for eight and the flush for twelve.

Afterwards he told people that when Christie went to answer it, he sat there and knew that the message was for him, and he knew what it was. He looked at the four spades and said to himself: I hope he's not killed.

His friend Archie, on his right at the square dining-room table, was humming the Kyrie Eleison. Any other time, Christie, Archie's mother, when she came back would say, "Archie, for God's sake stop that mournful noise," but this time, Ian knew, she would not. Across the table Archie's father drummed his fingers on the table and said, "You fellahs better have good pegging cards, if you don't want to be skunked." Another time Ian would have said, "You said it, partner." But this time he stared at his spades.

There was no telephone in his own house and the ring always sounded to him like an explosion, and every time he heard it, he expected it would bring news of his father's death. When he heard Christie's voice diminish, and say to the telephone, "Ian's here now, mumble mumble mumble," he thought, "I knew it. I knew it when it rang."

"There's an accident in 25," Christie said. She put her hand on Ian's shoulder. He stared at his spades and waited. "Two men are killed and two men are hurt."

"My father is one of the four?"

"Yes."

"Are they up?"

"Mrs. McLeod it was that called. She didn't know if they were up yet or not."

"Okay. I better go."

"You want me to drive you?" Archie said.

"No. I'll run home. My cousin is visiting. Her husband will take me out."

"Good luck," Christie said.

"Thanks," he said, and ran off in the dark.

There was a good chance his mother didn't know yet. Someone would have to call a neighbour. The neighbour would have to run over. They'd want to wait until they had definite news. He started to run faster. He was glad they didn't have a telephone. What a way to find out, especially if Johnny and Daisy were gone. If they were gone he'd have to get someone else to drive him. He slowed down to a walk. He didn't have far to go but it was pitch black. The road was rocky. He had been playing cards at his friends the Mac-Neils, who lived across the highway in the newest of co-op housing groups. Once across the highway there were lights and the road was graded and he started running, but he was soon near his driveway, the first one, in the oldest of the co-op housing groups. He walked the short driveway slowly, so he wouldn't be huffing and puffing going to the house.

His mother stood at the stove when he opened the door; in one hand she held the lifter with the cover hooked onto it, in the other hand she held the poker and was thrusting it into the burning coal.

"Well, you're back," she said. "Want a cup of tea? I'm just about to put some on."

"You didn't hear the news?"

"News. What news? Oh my God. Your father."

"They called MacNeils. I came right up."

"He's dead?"

"I don't think so."

"I think he's dead."

"There were four in it. Two are dead. But two are just hurt. I think Dad's just hurt."

"Oh God. I can't believe it."

"I better go and find out," he said. Johnny came out and offered to take him in his truck.

"Thanks," Ian said.

"Where'll we go?" Johnny said. "The pit or the hospital?"

"Better go to the pit first. They mightn't have them up yet. And even so we don't know what hospital. If they were bad off they might just go to the closest."

Ian expected a big crowd to be milling around the pit head, but there was nobody. It had started to drizzle. Johnny stopped the truck in the middle of the yard near the wash-house. The lights on the poles seemed able to light up only themselves; the buildings were soft shadows and in the wet dark seemed larger than they were. The door slammed shut. The man diminished to a shadow and disappeared around the corner. "We might as well go in there," Ian said.

Ian pulled open the door and stepped in. The room was steamy and crowded. A few men were still in their pit clothes, a few in their street clothes. Most were naked, half of them blackfaced with coal dust, the other half had finished showering and were pulling their street clothes down on the ropes and pulleys that kept them near the roofbeams while the men were in the pit. Ian wound his way through the crowd of men until he found a familiar face. "What happened, Frankie, where's Dad?"

"He's at St. Joseph's. They just left."

"We didn't pass them."

"They probably went the Sydney Road way. You must of come through Rabbit Town."

"Is he all right?"

"I don't know. He's hurt pretty bad. Likely he'll be all right. He was hunched down next to the machine. He got squeezed in the wedge but I think it saved him. Peter got killed."

"Peter?"

"Peter your cousin. He just started workin' with your father."

"Oh God."

"Roddie got killed."

"MacEachern?"

"Yeah. And Joe got hurt, don't know how bad. They took him off in the same truck with your father. They had the priest out for the other two. I heard him say St. Joseph's."

"Okay, I better get down there."

"Tell your father I'll be down later."

Inside the hospital front door the receptionist told him "down them steps straight ahead, right at the bottom is the room." At the bottom step he saw the family doctor come out a doorway facing the stair.

"How is he?"

"Touch and go," he said, and fled down the hall. "So far so good," he said over his shoulder and went through a doorway.

Ian went in. There was nothing in it but his father on his back, knees up, and a bed with steel legs and big rubber wheels. He was just as they pulled him out. The right leg of his pants was ripped to the knee. A gash like a long mouth full of blood and coal dust ran from knee to ankle. The ankle looked like a bone sticking out of a roast. The right arm of his shirt was off. The arm was black where it wasn't blue. His hands were on his belly palms down, the tips of his middle fingers touching. His face was black where it wasn't red. His hair was full of blood.

"Hello, Dada," Ian said. His father moved his black middle fingers and his blue eyes.

"How bad is it?" His father beckoned him down with his black index finger. Ian put his ear down close to his father's mouth.

"The son of a whore got me by the throat," he said. "Say a prayer, eh."

"I will."

"Put your head up now. I can talk loud enough. I didn't think I could." The voice was strong but whispery and gurgly. Ian straightened up.

"Does your mother know?"

"Yes, but she doesn't know yet if you're hurt or dead."

"Tell her I'll be okay. I think I can beat the son of a whore."

"Okay, just a minute. Johnny's out there. He drove me down. I'll go tell him to go up and tell them. I'll stay here." He went to the door and found Johnny sitting on the steps.

"How is he?"

"Don't know. Hurt bad but he'll be okay I think. I'm gonna stay. Would you go and tell Mother? Tell her he's gonna be okay. He'll be in for a while, but he'll be okay."

Back in the room, Ian found his father unconscious. His eyes were closed but his mouth was open, the teeth clenched and the lips pulled back in a grimace. There must be some other way a person could make a living, Ian thought. His father's eyes opened.

"You're back," he said.

"Yes."

"Was I out long?"

"No. Just a minute."

"Ian."

"Yeah."

"My feet are awful sore. Would you take off the boots?"

"Okay," Ian said and went to the foot of the bed and started to unlace the boots when he was startled by a harsh female voice.

"What are you doing?"

"Takin' off his boots."

"Who are you?"

"I'm Ian. His son."

"Oh, okay, take out the laces. But don't move the feet. I see he's unconscious again." She was only a few years older than Ian but she talked as if she owned the hospital. "I'm Sister Magdelene of the Holy Eucharist," she said, and pulled the foot-long pair of scissors out of a holster at her hip and took a few snips at the air over her shoulder.

"What's wrong with him?"

"Nothing much," she said. "His back is broke. Four broken ribs. He might have a rib stickin' a lung. His head is split, his spinal cord might be injured. Broken ankle, twisted knee plus a million cuts and bruises. My guess is he'll live. But x-rays will tell the tale. Have you got the laces out?"

"One."

"Okay, do the other," she said and she took the scissors and cut all the buttons off the shirt, then snipped it across the chest. She opened his belt, cut open his fly, snipped the pants across, then up the legs, folded everything back, slashed at both legs of his father's boxer shorts until finally everything but the shoes were in rags, hanging down from the sides of the bed and his father lay stark naked, his penis hard and sticking straight up in the air.

"See that," she said, "I told you he'd live. They're often like that after an accident," she said. "It's because they think they're going to heaven. Did you finish the laces?"

Ian stared between his father's knees. He couldn't get his mouth going to say yes.

"Don't be embarrassed," she said, "I'm used to it. I used to be a whore, before I entered the convent. I guess that's why they put me down here." She came to the end of the bed and went to work with the scissors on the shoes. "You go to the next room," she said, "and bring in the pan of water by the sink and start washing him. Once we get him clean we can cover him up and up he goes. Go ahead now, this kind of thing is easier on you if you keep busy and keep talking so you don't get mopey."

When they finished they put him, bed and all, covered with a sheet, on the elevator. "Sister Mary'll look after him now," she said to Ian, "won't you, Sister Mary?"

"Yes," Sister Mary said through the elevator door. She smiled.

"They won't let me up there," Sister Magdelene of the Holy Eucharist said. "They're scared I'll say something dirty and disgrace the order. Isn't that it, Sister Mary?"

"Yes," said Sister Mary. She smiled.

"How about you stay here and help me with the other one," she said to Ian. "You might as well while you're waiting. C'mon, his two legs are broke—he might be cranky."

The other one was Joe the Pig Two MacDonald. The name he inherited from his father, also Joe MacDonald, nicknamed to distinguish him from the dozen or so other Joseph MacDonalds, most of whom had somewhat weaker distinctions such as D.P., Joe D., ABCD and so on, and because he once pronounced to his buddies, during a tea-break in the pit, one of the few general conclusions he had distilled from forty years of living: "You know," he said, "a man had a good pig, he wouldn't be in the need of a wife."

It turned out Joe the Pig Two was not cranky. He was sore, exhausted and astonished at his good luck, having once again escaped death. His mood shifted between sorrow when he thought of his two dead buddies, and happiness when he thought of himself and Angus and their wives and all their kids.

"Watch them scissors, Maggie," he said to Sister Magdelene. "My wife'll be down to inspect and if she finds anything missing she'll be fit to be tied."

"Don't worry, me b'y, it's only your legs'll be shorter. The rest of you'll be all right."

"You don't mean that. My legs."

"No no no. Just kiddin'. They won't need to cut them off."

"How is Angus makin' out?"

"Gone up for x-rays. I think he'll be good."

"Thank Christ. Them other two didn't have a fuckin' hope. Excuse me, Sister."

"It's okay."

"What happened, anyway, Joe?" Ian said.

"Whole goddamn roof came down on us. I heard 'er crack and jumped for the door. Got everything out but the last of my legs. Broke both, crushed a foot. Your father was hunched down by the machine. Saved him. Held up one side of the stone enough. He was crushed in there but it was enough room. Peter and Roddie were in deeper. Flattened like pancakes. Your father said that roof was no good before we started. Too late now."

"Now turn over on your belly," Sister Magdelene of the Holy Eucharist said and Joe the Pig Two turned over and she began to wash his back.

"Could I ask you a question, Sister?"

"Ask away."

"Well, I got two questions," he said. "One is, how much would you charge a week to do this every day? And the other is, would you make house calls?"

"You don't shut up," she said, "I'm goin' for the scissors again. Ian would you go and change the water. I think it's makin' him worse."

THE COFFINS AT BOTH FUNERALS were closed. At Roddie the Log MacEachern's wake the children were all grown, the widow sedate and the wake was calm, sombre and formal. It was Ian's first Protestant funeral, and once in the little front-room where the mourners were gathered he discovered there was no kneeling bench, and since the coffin was closed, he felt silly standing there looking at its brown curved top. So he knelt anyway, thinking that no one could object to a prayer, even a Catholic prayer. But with all the Protestant eyes arrayed around the room he couldn't bring himself to make the sign of the cross and finally in his confusion he didn't even pray; he held his hands together on his belt buckle and studied the curlicues on the burnished brass handles of the box.

Before getting to his feet he tried to figure out where he could go next. Most times he simply said a prayer and left unless it was a wake of a close relative. But this time he felt he was here as a representative of the family, for his father who was still in the hospital, for his mother who was still reeling and for his brothers and sister who would come too but who were younger than himself and still officially children. He noticed that the regular living-room furniture had been removed and replaced by kitchen chairs and card-table chairs, which were lined around the walls. The people in them were not looking at him at all, but quietly talking or looking at their hands, knees or feet. He spotted some empty spaces and walked over and sat. The widow, Mrs. MacEachern, came and sat beside him.

"Thank you for coming, Ian," she said.

"That's okay," he said, "I'm sorry it happened." It was what his mother told him to say. "How are you feeling?"

She wore a black dress with a black belt and silver buckle, and black shoes and a bit of black hat with a black veil hanging from it over her eyes. It was the first time he had seen a veil on a grown woman. Behind the veil her eyes were quiet and blank as if concentrating intently on some unimportant distraction.

"I'm fine for now," she said. "How is your father?"

"Well, he's very sore, but they're saying he'll be okay."

"And Joseph, too, will recover?"

"Yes."

"His legs are broken?"

"Yes," Ian said.

"He'll be better soon."

"Yes."

"How long will your father be in the hospital?"

"I don't know. At least a month, I guess."

"Does he get up?"

"No, not yet."

"How is your mother?"

"She hasn't gotten over it yet. She's still not sure he's going to get better."

"Poor thing," she said. "Well, at least in the end, she'll have him back."

"Yes, that's true."

"Have you been to Peter's wake?"

"No. I'm going after."

"I was over before," she said. "Poor Gloria is taking it awful hard."

"I heard that, but I wasn't over yet."

"You can't talk to her."

"I heard she can't stop crying."

"She can't. She can't help it. She does stop sometimes, but the minute you start to talk to her, or she tries to talk to you, she starts to sob."

"They say she doesn't sleep," he said.

"She'll doze off. But she hasn't left the room to sleep or eat. She won't leave the room. She sits there and every now and again she gets up and goes over and puts her hand on the coffin. It's closed, you know, same as Roddie's. She goes back and sits. She won't leave the room."

"Yes. I heard that."

"She's young though," Mrs. MacEachern said. "She'll get over it. Next week she'll stop."

"Yes," Ian said. "She's young. She has two babies."

"Yes. Next week she'll stop," Mrs. MacEachern said. "And when she stops, then I'll start."

Ian felt he should say something reassuring, but he couldn't think of anything. He looked through the veil at her fearful eyes. "This week," she said, "I'm talking to people. I hope they don't mind."

"I'm sure no one minds," Ian said. "Everyone knows how hard it is."

"Yes. We're all used to it. We know how hard it is. I always see you going back and forth to school. Ever since you moved up Sydney Road. But this is the first chance I had to talk to you."

"That's right," Ian said. "I still don't know many peo-ple up this way."

"Do you know my Roddie's nickname?"

"Yes."

"Do you know how he got it?"

"No. I never heard," Ian said, although he had. He wanted to hear her version.

"When the kids were little, we had a fire. We were in the company house then, up in Reserve Rows. I was right there when it happened, in the kitchen, having a cup of tea with my sister, Marie, but I don't know yet how it got start-ed. The wall behind the stove broke into flames. It was hot, I guess. The middle of July. I was baking bread. Three of the kids were sick upstairs having a nap. The baby was in the front room. Marie ran for the fire department. This was just after they got their truck. I got all the kids out and the men came and put out the fire. The place was a mess. Water all over the kitchen. When the smoke cleared we cleaned it up and sat down to our tea again. The kids were all excited, the baby was crying. It started again. They had to come again and put it out. This time they had to rip open the wall. This time we took the kids over to Marie's. We had our tea there. An hour later there's a knock at the door and who comes in but Roddie. 'Flora,' he said, 'what's goin' on? There's water all over the kitchen floor.' Well we laughed to kill ourselves. I forgot what shift he was on. I thought he was at work. He slept through the two fires. Never even knew they happened. But I thought afterwards.

He could have been burned alive and I wouldn't have known, thinking he was all the time at work. Of course when your father heard that, he said now that's what I call sleeping like a log. I felt guilty for years thinking I could have as good as killed him. Now he's dead anyway. He was an awful good man. Thank God it wasn't me that killed him. Come on to the kitchen, Ian, and have a cup of tea and a bite. They called him the Log ever since. Roddie the Log MacEachern."

"Thanks," Ian said. "I might have a cup."

Fortified with tea and pieces of ham, Ian walked down the Sydney Road past the corner where it met Main Street to the rows of company houses in the Lorway. He didn't know the house but he kept on until he saw the wreath beside the front door. He had known Peter and he knew Gloria. They had been in the same grade together. He had walked with her the mile or so to school every day when they lived in Reserve Rows. Peter, who lived in Rabbit Town, walked down the tram-car tracks and joined them every day where the tracks and Main Street came together. Ian courted her as far as there, in his indirect fashion, every day. He had to stop it there because she was Peter's girl. She knew he was courting her but he did it so she could know it and not acknowledge it. She never acknowledged it. "I'm telling you this," she said, "as if you were my brother, because I know you won't breathe a word. I'm going to marry Peter, or I'm going to be a nun."

"Gloria in excelsis Deo," he said.

"Yes," she said, "or Peter."

"What about Gloria in excelsis Ian?"

"Nope," she said. "It's God or Peter."

"I'm pulling for God," Ian said.

"Well, I'm pulling for Peter, tell you the truth," she said.

When she became pregnant, God dropped out of the competition. "I'm glad," she told Ian. "I'm not cut out for a nun, anyway. I just love Sister Immaculata and her servabo me servato te. I'd like to be able to talk like that, but I know I'm not cut out for it. You maybe, but not me. I'll be sorry to quit though. Peter'll have to quit too. He doesn't like school a lot, but he's doing okay."

"Will you finish the year?"

"I think I will, if I don't get too big. Peter thinks he'll be hired on right away. If he is he's gonna quit."

"Will you tell Sister Immaculata?"

"I think I'll just let her find out. I wonder what she'll say?"

"I know what she'll say," Ian said.

"What?"

"She'll say passer mortuus est meae pullae."

"What does that mean?"

"It means you better get ready to do your own flying."

When Ian arrived at Peter's wake the priest and the nuns were there, all kneeling in front of chairs around the wall saying the rosary. Gloria was sitting in a corner in a stuffed chesterfield chair her mother had brought back into the front room, hoping that its comfort would seduce her to sleep. She sat at the front edge of it, her elbows on her knees, her face in her hands. Her sobs were dry.

They were beginning the first Sorrowful Mystery, "The Agony in the Garden."

Ian knelt on the kneeling-bench in front of the coffin and looked at the brown polished wood. After he said a few prayers he saw there was no convenient place to go in the small room; people were kneeling out in the middle of the floor as well as in the front of the chairs at the wall, so he stayed on the bench in front of the coffin and joined in the prayers, led by the priest. "Hail Mary, full of Grace, the Lord is with thee, blessed art thou among women and blessed is the fruit of thy womb...."

Because he couldn't see Peter's face in the coffin, his head filled with images of Peter in their common past. He and Peter hunting squirrels with their slingshots; digging a bootleg pit, thinking they would make a fortune selling coal and take a trip to Boston to see their cousins; swimming naked in the icy May water in the So'West Brook; walking out to Dominion Beach in the hot summer to dash into the icy ocean, three miles of walking with the gang and telling dirty jokes, and after swimming, sitting around the beach, talking to the girls, and trying to be mature; Peter sliding into second base and standing up in one motion; Peter scoring a goal with a backhand shot over the goalie's shoulder after he thought Peter had made the turn around the net; Peter racking up 56 points off the break to start a winning streak; playing snooker for three months with the same quarter in his pocket; he had it so long, he said, that he rubbed the king off one side and the moose off the other, so when he finally lost a game, Joe thought it was a slug and wouldn't take it, so he had to owe him for the time. Peter pulling out an unexpected pint of rum when they were taking the short cut home after the dance, saying, "Have a slug a black death," and passing it back and forth, and throwing the empty in a high arc over the trees, and standing there, his penis gleaming in the moonlight, saying, "Have a sluga white death," and Ian saying, "No thanks, I just had an orange." And laughing.

Ian, without thinking, lifted his hands from his belt buckle and put them on the edge of the brown coffin. I was always a little jealous, he thought. I have to admit it. He always had been, a little, because although Ian made the slingshots, and invented the use of marbles instead of rocks, which tended to veer off target, it was Peter who dared to make a present of the squirrel's tail to the girls they lusted after and to tell them: "You wear them where we'll have to look for them." It was Ian who'd say, "The So'West must be pretty good by now," but it was Peter who knifed into it from a tree without even testing the water with his toe, scattering the surprised trout, taking a long slow swim underwater, and climbing out, red-skinned from head to toe. "Warm as toast," he'd say. You had to admire that. He had envied him. But not much or for long because he thought of him as a brother. More than a brother because sometimes you could hate your brother. "Holy Mary, Mother of God, pray for us sinners, now and at the hour of our death, amen. Glory be to the Father and to the Son and to the Holy Ghost."

"Amen."

"De profundis clamo ad te, Domine."

"Domine audi vocem meam." Everyone got up off their knees and sat in the chairs around the wall and prayed in silence, or chatted. Some went out to the kitchen for a cup of tea and to talk. At a wake, there are always people you never see any other time. Ian left the kneeling-bench in front of the coffin and walked over to Gloria's chair and sat on the arm. She was seated at the front edge of it as she was when he came in, her face in her hands. He put his finger on her shoulder.

"Hello, Gloria," he said. She took her face out of her hands and put her thumbs under her chin and turned her head.

"Ian. I'm glad you came."

"How are you doing?"

"Terrible. Just terrible. My mother has to do everything! I should be doing things but every time I start even to talk I start to cry."

"You seem better now."

"Yes. This is the first time. The first dry words since they brought him home in that box. I didn't cry till then. I didn't believe it till then. But look, my eyes are dry now." They were dry, and brown, and large and round. Her ordeal

had not harmed her beauty. If anything, she was better looking than he remembered. She was still small, but seemed
more substantial, and dressed in black, she seemed older.
Ian remembered her ambition to become a nun. All she
needs now, he thought, is a cowl and a longer dress and
she'd be one of the nuns who came to pray at her husband's
wake.

"You look awful tired," he said.

"I am tired. I haven't slept since they brought him
home."

"Why don't you go up and lie down for a while now?"

"Will you take me up?"

"Sure," he said, and they stood up, as if he had asked
her to dance, and they faced each other for a moment. Sister
Immaculata came over and put her gentle hands on their
arms.

"I'm terribly sorry, Gloria, you've had such trouble."

"Thank you, Sister. It's awful, but I'll get over it; at
least they tell me that."

"That's right, you know. You'll never forget it but
you'll feel better as time goes by."

"She's going to go up and lie down for a while," Ian
said.

"Oh that's good, Gloria, have a good rest. You'll need
it."

Upstairs, lying on her back, her long brown hair
splayed on the white pillow, she started to cry again as Ian
looked down at her and tried to smile reassurance.

"Would you sit down beside me for a minute, Ian?"
He sat.

"Would you hold my hand?" He took her hand and
held it on his thigh. Her eyes watered. "Can I tell you something?" she said.

"Yes."

"The last thing I said to him, I said: 'If you never come
back, I don't give a shit!'"

"How come?"

"We were having an argument. About nothing, of
course."

"Well, you didn't mean it."

"No. But my God I said it."

"He'd know you didn't mean it."

"I feel guilty."

"You know you didn't mean it."

"I loved him."

"He'd have known that. He'd know you didn't mean
it."

"Can I tell you something else, Ian?"

"Yes."

"I loved you a little too. Did you know that?"

"Yes."

"I couldn't tell you."

"I know."

"I feel guilty about that too."

"It doesn't matter if you feel it. You didn't do anything wrong. The feeling will go away."

"I hope so," she said. "I loved the both of you." She lifted her black dress and black slip and lifted Ian's hand and placed it on the round of her belly, above the tops of her black stockings. His hand jerked in panic, but she said, "Don't worry, Ian, I wouldn't hurt you, be still. I just want it there to breathe against." She closed her eyes and almost at once began to breathe deeply, her bosom rising and falling rhythmically, and her hands clasped together calmly on his. Ian watched his hand slowly rising and falling. Then her hands lay beside her on the brown, brocaded bedspread, palms up, as if in supplication. He became aware of silence, and then he could hear that the prayers had started again downstairs. "...blessed is the fruit of thy womb...." He wondered how anyone could wear garters tight around the legs; he couldn't stand even the elastics of stockings. "...pray for us sinners, now, and at the hour of our death...." He waited until he heard the final words: "Requiem aeternam dona ei, Domine: Ex lux perpetua luceat ei," then he pulled his hand free, pulled Gloria's slip and dress over her knees, covered her with a quilt from the foot of the bed, walked downstairs, smiled and nodded at Sister Immaculata when she asked in a whisper if she was asleep. He went home.

The Party

IAN STRETCHED OUT in the upstairs hall next to the vent over the furnacette where he could keep his ear and occasionally his eye on the party below. He had his pencil and scribbler next to him with the names of everyone below written down and next to the names the number of drinks each one had, the number of times each went to the outhouse and what each one said, leaving out comments on the weather, the price of jam and the dresses of the ladies present unless they were interesting and he hadn't heard them before, such as, "That's nice material, Mary, you should have a dress made out of it," or, "I couldn't give her candy for Christmas so I gave her nuts for New Year's," or "Cold enough to freeze the hinge off the shit-house door," and, of course, all items referring to himself: "For God's sake, Angus, watch your tongue. You know that boy is up half the night reading."

"I don't think he can hear from his room."

"He can hear anything he has a mind to."

"Let him hear," Roddie said. "He needs the education. He won't get it in school."

In the middle of the scribbler he wrote his own version of what was happening downstairs under the title "The

Bearcat" which was the puzzling name printed on the cover of his scribbler along with the puzzling drawing of a big brown bear on his hind legs holding a rather impractical hockey stick. So far the name had nothing to do with the story, "but it soon might," he whispered to himself.

The Bearcat

"DID YOU NOTICE," he said to his female companion at his elbow, huddled with him behind the chesterfield, her burgeoning breast bulging against its slim prison and softly caressing the hair on his upper limb on which he had short sleeves, "that the men go out more than the women." He moved his arm a little as he spoke.

"Yes," came the riposte, couched in a whisper so as not to give away their cachement.

"By close observations and clever calculation," he offered, triumphantly, "I have concluded that the goings out are directly proportioned to the drinkings in."

"Ah, that makes sense," was her respectful reply, edging a little closer and making the little hairs on his upper arm stand up and quiver in ecstasy. She was the daughter, Morag by name, a fine full name that for a girl who, as yet a slip of a thing, held the promise in her developing physique of full bodied pulchritude. She was the daughter in fact of the man now speaking. She had an effect on Rob Roy out of proportion to her as yet plainness.

"You can say, Angus, what you like when you're drinking, but like the fella says," (it was a phrase he used ad nau-

seam) *"where're you gonna buy stuff when the store ain't there."*

"Their prices are good, you have to admit, isn't that right, Cathy?" Tina cut in. *"Take jam. Lizzy told me what she paid for jam in town. Their prices are good,"* she repeated, *unnecessarily. "You got to admit that don't you, Catherine?"*

Catherine would not admit it. In point of fact she agreed with Tina and were they by themselves in one or the other's kitchens she might have nodded so as not to appear rude, but she would not go against her husband in public, even after a hot shine and sugar and the alcohol coursing through her veins and suffusing her loins. She often argued the point herself but only in bed or some other private place where in the end she could reach out and smooth the difference between them, caressing it into ecstatic oblivion. But in public she was adamant in her refusal to fly in the face of her husband's wishes, to flag in support of her man, a quality appreciated by her son but probably not noticed by her spouse, who was more concerned with politics and external affairs.

"Never mind the price of goddamn jam, Tina," Roddie expostulated.

"Well, what are we talking about if not the price of jam?" she returned.

"We're talking about stores not bottles," came the impatient riposte.

"What do they sell in stores?" she queried, not to be so easily repulsed now she was a little tipsy. *"Jam,"* she answered her own question, *"jam, jam, jam."*

"*Oh. Be quiet, Tina.*"

"*Be quiet me arse,*" *she returned, not so sensitive to her husband's image as her companion, and turning her daughter's face behind the chesterfield crimson. Catherine reached over and touched her on the wrist and whispered tentatively in her ear. "Take care. My boy stays up half the night in his bed reading. He can hear every word if he has a mind to.*"

"*Thank God my Morag goes to bed early,*" *came the thick reply, causing a sudden renewal of blushing behind the chesterfield. "That's what stores are about—the price of jam," she reiterated.*

"*What Angus is talking about is the kind of store that belongs to the people themselves, not the company or the Jews.*"

"*Oh my God, now he's gonna start in on the Jews again,*" *she wailed. This was their constant argument. Who is to blame for their sad lot? Rob Roy began to feel sorry for his female companion, Morag, sitting quietly beside him behind the chesterfield showing no overt sign of the embarrassment that must be hers. Perhaps he shouldn't have asked her over. As a token of his sympathy he placed his hand on her raised knees; she drew them apart slightly and let his index finger slip slightly between, to demonstrate her understanding of his gesture. He traced his index finger briefly over the soft downy flesh. She gently squeezed her knees together, holding for a moment his appendage in its tender trap between her legs. Their heads turned toward each other, simultaneously, and their gazes met. The room beyond the chesterfield vanished in their moment of quiet ecstasy.*

But not for long. Rudely the routine conversation re-turned. "Isn't that what the priest said, what's his name?"

"Coady."

"No—the other one. What'd he say? Food first."

"If your belly's full, then you can talk about other things."

"That's not what he said."

"Well what did he say then?"

"He said up to now decisions are made by people who eat banquets, not by people who eat out of lunch cans."

"Well, that's the same goddamn thing."

"Shh. Shh."

"It's not the same goddamn thing."

"Well it's pretty near."

"Anyway what Angus is talking about is who runs the bloody store not what price they charge for jam, for Christ's sake."

Morag gave an involuntary start when she again heard her father take the Lord's name in vain. Ian's hand slipped involuntarily down between her raised legs, over the soft white flesh. Neither of them appeared to notice, so intent they seemed on the outcome of the heated discussion in the front room in front of their hideout.

"Does he have to have you to tell us what he means, the poor man if he does. Angus, could I have another little nip? What are you talking about anyway, Angus? You're awful quiet tonight."

"About owning the store," he said curtly.

"*Oh yes,*" *she said disdainfully, beginning to suspect she might be shown up to be on the losing end of the argument.* "*It's always them who haven't the price of a bottle of jam that talks about buying the store.*"

Morag gave Ian's hand a squeeze to indicate that she thought her mother had a good point. Ian simply waited for his father's reply, which he knew would be devastating were it not for the fact he was addressing himself to a lady, albeit a tipsy lady.

"*It's not a question,*" *came the subdued tones,* "*of me buying a store.*"

"*What is the question anyway?*" *asked Roddie, thickly. He too was beginning to feel the effects of the alcohol.*

"*Yes,*" *Catherine said, smiling to be sure her husband knew she was joking.* "*Tell us once again, for the umpteenth time what it's a question of.*"

Angus was visibly embarrassed by his wife's remark in spite of her sweetening smile and he replied uncertainly.

"*Well isn't that it,*" *said he enigmatically.* "*The whole thing is right there.*"

"*What whole thing?*" *Tina put in, disdainfully.*

"*We talk and talk and talk,*" *Angus said sadly. Behind the chesterfield the young man and his female companion were divided between listening to this oft-repeated discussion they were hearing in its entirety for the first time, and their blossoming sexual relationship. His hand between the firm white flesh of her thighs had gone to sleep but he was reluctant to pull it loose for fear she would misinterpret his gesture.*

"We talk and talk and talk," his father repeated. "And we laugh at ourselves for talking so much about it. But when we finish talking and laughing and drinking everything is the same. They own the store, they own the house, they own the pits. You can't even dig a hole in your own backyard but it's against the law."

The lad behind the chesterfield felt like clapping for this speech but one of his clappers was asleep in its trap. Indeed his hand had jerked in an involuntary movement, but his female companion only squeezed all the tighter and gave him a knowing look.

"Well," said Tina, indignant, "what the hell is a person expected to do? They got us by the you know what," she continued in the language of the streets. "We can't do anything. We got no money," she said pathetically.

"Worse than that," Roddie cut in, "we got to work next week to pay for what we ate last week."

"I'll be back in a while," Angus said abruptly.

"Where?" Catherine queried.

"Down the road," he replied.

"Oh Angus. Don't go," said she.

"I need cigarettes," he said.

"Here," Johnny said, "I have the makin's."

"No," Angus responded. "I feel like a tailor-made."

"Oh, Angus. Don't get more shine," Catherine said worriedly. "We have enough."

"I'll go with you," Roddie suggested.

"No," Angus said. "Keep the women company. I won't be

long. The Little Store might not be open anyway. I'll be right back," he said and left before anyone could say another word.

In the absence of Angus the conversation was very boring to those left in the living-room and equally to those in their hiding place behind the chesterfield who, of course, had amusement other than eavesdropping on a desultory conversation.

But first he had to get his hand out. He couldn't risk a whisper during a lull in conversation so he waited and finally Tina said, "I don't care what they say everybody says, even Angus says, you're gonna go where you get the best price and when you've got no money you have to go where they'll put it on tick."

"My hand is asleep."

"Oh," she made an O with her mouth and ducked her head in a sheepish grin and loosened the velvet trap of her thighs. Immediately he began to work on his hand to rid it of its pins and needles.

"It's true," Catherine ventured in her husband's absence. "You go downtown and every store has a different price and they're all higher than the company store."

"Or if not," Tina continued, directing her remarks to her husband as if he had just made a point she was about to triumphantly dispute, although he had not said a word, and indeed was on the point of dozing off, the argument being Tina's familiar form of speech, "you don't get the quality or they don't give you enough."

Morag had taken Ian's hand and began to knead it, no

more efficaciously than his own ministrations, but neverthe-less he found the sensation not unpleasant.

AT THIS POINT Ian changed his character's name from Rob Roy to Leslie after his favourite author, and in the back of his mind began to consider more suitable names for his other characters. Whoever heard of Angus in a story? he thought. Catherine might be okay but I might change it to Aragon but I'll have to find something better than groceries for them to talk about. Whoever heard of a story about groceries. In the meantime, he thought, I'll just get it down in the scribbler. I'm getting too dozy to do it right now.

"I KNOW," Catherine said. "They sometimes give you way over what you pay for. Specially when Angus goes to the store. Sometimes you get a pound and a half almost for one. It's a little bit dishonest you know."

"For the love of Jesus Mary and Joseph you two would drive a man to Sydney River," said Roddie, a little piqued at his wife for throwing her words at him, and feeling he should take Angus's part now he wasn't here.

"What are you talking about?" his wife responded.

Behind the chesterfield Morag, emboldened by her kneading of his hand, began to feel she needed something more. She delicately unbuttoned the top button of his shirt and when she had finished she smiled at her work as if contemplating the beginning of a long pleasant journey. Ian felt a sense of urgency course through his veins.

"What I'm talking about," Roddie said emphatically, "is that you're not talkin' about what Angus is talkin' about at all."

"I suppose you know what everybody is talking about."

"Well I know what he's talkin' about. God knows I listen to it every day of my life I go to work. He's talkin' about owning the goddamn things that you're all the time paying for."

"Oh yeah. It's nice talk."

"Well," he said, firmly, but he was not sure how to go on. "You have to talk first. You have to listen. You have to know what to do…."

"Do what?" she cut in.

"Like the fella says, the poor man has to be organized, he can't do nothin' alone."

"Do what?" she insisted.

"Whatever needs to be done," he said vaguely.

"What needs to be done?"

"Well," he said, more firmly now, "we need to build our own store and our own houses."

"Sure," she said, contemptuously. "We'll start tomorrow. With what?"

By now Ian's belly button was exposed. Morag put her little finger in it and looked into his face and smiled as if to indicate her utter joy at finding such an extraordinary, such a perfect, such a transcendental button hidden among a row of such ordinary, such plain, such common buttons, some of them so damaged from scrubbing that they hardly any longer *served their mundane purpose. She extracted a piece of lint with her little finger and wiped it off on his belt buckle, and looked into his face again, as if to say, what further exciting discoveries might not be made by an intrepid explorer pushing back the pregnant frontiers of this virgin territory.*

"Money," Roddie said. "You got to have money."

"Of course you have to have money," Tina expostulated. "Why don't we borrow it against what we owe the company store," she continued, again with contempt.

"Well, I don't know," he confessed. "That's what those priests say, we can get it if we get organized. They must know something. They're at the university."

"Yes. And guess who's paying their salaries?"

"Well now, Tina, you know they don't get much."

"Sure but where do they get it?"

"They get it from the diocese."

"And where do they get it? They get it from you and Angus. And they don't look hungry to me."

"Well, we're not hungry yet."

"And what do they do? What do they do? What do they do? They talk, they talk, they talk. Just like you and me. So long as their bellies are full. And when their bellies are not full they'll start kicking. Just like you and me. What we need are people who can kick when their bellies are full while they have the strength to kick hard."

Behind the chesterfield Morag looked up from her ministrations to smile proudly to indicate to him she thought her mother's speech was pretty good, but Ian was all together too excited to reciprocate the smile and barely contained himself by sucking in his breath between his teeth, noiselessly. He heard the door slam. Angus must be home. What if someone should look behind the chesterfield? He heard Angus's steps.

"Did you have any luck?" Roddie called.

"Angus, my God, Angus, what's the matter?"

"The company store is on fire."

The Path

WHEN HE SAW THE FLASH, Spider MacDougall was sitting in his front room staring across the street at the window of the company store. It had snowed the day before and between his front gate and the front yard of the store across the street the white blanket had been systematically broken into a thin path by the uncountable steps of his brood. It was Spider's custom to sit in his front room every Saturday afternoon after his nap; first to read a newspaper and then to follow the many travelers of the path back and forth, through snow in winter, and mud in the spring and fall. Even the hard baked clay of summer yielded, and the practiced eye could detect in it a line left by the ceaseless trek.

Spider was a small, short, thin, wiry, tightly packed, muscular, large-chested man with arms and legs full of hair and veins. If God, God forgive him, had had coal miners in mind when he started the world, Spider might have been his model. He was small enough to stand up under all but the lowest roof, and his powerful arms could load coal twice as fast or twice as long as any man around. His body was without fat; everything he ate turned to work.

He quit school and started in the pit as a trapper when he was eleven to help his mother feed the family after his fa-

79

ther died of a ton of rock on his back. But his strength was so phenomenal and his mother so poor that he was soon loading coal. His buddy was his cousin Archie, a man twice his age, of ordinary strength but of pride so fierce that he couldn't abide that a child could load more coal in a day than himself, or work more shifts in a week. So between them they astounded everybody and became a little bit rich.

He didn't smoke, or chew, or drink, and was too young to think of buying things for women; his only real pleasures in life were walking back and forth to work, snaring rabbits and making Archie work a little bit harder than was necessary; so he had little interest in his envelope which he turned over to his mother who, after she had clothed and fed her lot, took to wearing hats and buying teacups.

In spite of his age, his opulence created a curiosity in several young ladies who now and again tried what custom and tradition would permit to attract his attention, but to little avail. He wouldn't go to a dance. He didn't know why not. He had the energy; his work by no means exhausted his resources. He simply couldn't see the use of it. If he went to a party, he left early out of boredom. He often worked an extra shift, and he seldom left his house without a specific destination, so his general availability was limited. The best bet was to walk home with him after church, a tactic several ladies tried but soon gave up, exasperated. Spider was not a talker.

Madeline Boyd, however, had no trouble at all. She was a plump girl and not pretty in the accepted style, so she was accustomed to getting her own way by careful planning.

Directly across from the company store, where, at the time Madeline worked as a clerk, Spider lived in one half of a duplex company house surrounded by a painted picket fence. Even then he sat on Saturdays in the living room and looked blankly across the street at the store, until he could think of something useful to do. But there wasn't much he liked to do.

Baseball bored him and soon in the summer the heated colliery league contests between Reserve and Dominion and New Waterford and Glace Bay came to their victorious or heart-breaking conclusions without his applause or displeasure. They asked him to play. They knew he would be good. His knees were so close to the ground and his shoulders so close to his knees that only a pitcher with perfect control could ever strike him out even if he never swung a bat. They knew he had arms and shoulders and chest for slamming home runs into Belgium Town. They knew he was quick of hand and eye. His buddy Archie once bought a new .22 rifle and brought it over to show him. Spider stood in his front yard and in fifteen seconds killed six cats including his own off the roof, at distances ranging from twenty feet to three hundred yards.

"What d'ya think of her?" Archie said.

"That all she'll hold?" Spider said. "For the luva Jesus, Mother, shut up, it's only a fuckin' cat."

But when they asked him to play ball he said, "No, I don't think so, I'd rather go to the woods and snare rabbits."

"Well, just come once, and see what it's like."

"I know what it's like," he said. "It's like gardens. It's for the Eyetalians."

In the winter he wouldn't play hockey. "I can't skate," he said. But they knew he would be a good goalie because he was fearless.

"You don't need to skate to tend goal," they said.

"No," he said, "you don't, but you need to have skates."

"We'll lend you a pair," they said.

"They wouldn't fit," he said.

WHEN HE WAS LITTLE he played milk-can cricket in the spring and peggy in the fall, but without the enthusiasm, and he quit as soon as he heard about rabbit snaring. In the spring and summer he'd go fishing. Otherwise he'd sit in the front room and gaze across at the company store.

He could never figure out what Sunday was for. Other people, he noticed, had Sunday clothes and wore them to church and to ball games. And they'd walk home afterwards, a long line of talking, laughing people. He went a few times, walked home with people but he never heard anyone say anything worth laughing at. After a while he quit going to church altogether. "I don't know why they have Sunday at all," he said to his mother.

"Well, you enjoy the woods," she said.

"Yeah. It's alright for killin' things in. Outside that you might as well be in the pit or starin' at the store."

She never tried to force him to go to church, even as young as he was. "He has his own ways with him, that lad," she explained to herself, and consoled herself with hats.

Spider's occasional Sunday entertainment was a visit to his grandmother's. Sometimes she talked and sometimes she didn't, and she was satisfied to have him there and that satisfied him. The son that lived with her could go out when Spider was around and Spider had no other plans. And once, twice each visit, he'd hear her say, or she'd just bring it, "Here's some brown bread and black currant jam and a nice hot cup of tea."

Madeline Boyd studied his ways. He never twigged to the danger of the shapeless silhouette that crossed back and forth behind the big store window at the end of his gaze. His vision was too perfect to be wise.

He put off shaving as long as possible. He couldn't see the use of it. His father had taken great pleasure in shaving and had accumulated as gifts from his wife several elaborate articles designed to increase his pleasure in the ceremony. She had inherited a fancy mug from her father and she gave him that; and over the years she had given him as gifts several straight razors and brushes to celebrate his birthdays. All this paraphernalia, when the time came, she placed on her son's dresser. He ignored it as long as he could. But he thought a beard would be stupid and bothersome and finally gave in. "What an awful wasta time." In the mirror Spider could see only his face. It looked the same to him, except for a little blood.

One stormy Sunday afternoon in the winter he took his rabbit wire and a lunch and struck out for Rabbit Town.

"Are you goin' in this?" she said.

"It's the best time," he said.

"You'll perish."

"If it's too bad I'll stay in my shack the night. Night shift tomorrow. Don't have to be back till the afternoon." It was their usual conversation for the occasion.

He began to check his snares after he passed the last house in Rabbit Town. A trail started there and ran for two miles or so through the woods. He had built a cabin just before the end of the trail, about two hundred yards from it.

He had set his traps on Saturday evening. First he had studied the little trails, because as he tried to explain to his mother, "the little round turds show that the stupid little furry buggers were using the trail since the last snowfall and probably still are." Each snare was a noose which hung in the little rabbit trail. It was tied to a young poplar tree bent in a hoop and held down by a weakened rope. When Mr. Bunny put his head in the noose the rope broke, he went flying into the air and hung there until Sunday. On Sunday Spider collected the rabbits, repaired the snares, and left them hanging high to be set the next Saturday.

He collected about a dozen rabbits to be given to his mother or sold to the store. As he approached the cabin he saw smoke rising from the chimney. When he pushed open the door Madeline was cooking supper on the little stove.

After breakfast next morning they walked back together. Spider had not been easy to get along with at first, but she found that if she rubbed him the right way she got a fairly warm response. For her it had been a significant evening: flying in the face of the teaching of the church and the warnings of her mother could have dire consequences. But in the morning she felt peaceful. Except for a little blood, she appeared to herself to be exactly the same. Her companion seemed to have enjoyed himself. In the morning he was smiling. She had never seen him smile and she had been watching him pretty closely.

"I didn't think you liked it at first," she said.

"Well, tell you the truth, I never heard of it before. I didn't know what you were doing."

"You never heard of it before?"

"No. I just knew it of rabbits and dogs."

"In some things people are a lot like rabbits and dogs," she said.

"Probably the best part of them," he said.

WHEN THEY GOT MARRIED and Madeline moved in, Spider's mother moved out to live with her other son who now had a job in the mine. She would never be so rich. As for Madeline and Spider they had twelve babies, all of them apostles of Madeline. When she moved in with Spider she quit her job, but she never quite finished with the store across the street. She kept running back to it six or seven times a day until her children were old enough to walk; then she sent them. It was as if she'd forgotten something and kept sending back for it without success, or as if the store had some mysterious package they coveted but what they brought back always turned out to be the wrong thing.

"Nothin' in that store but bread," the children complained, but still, they kept returning. When they got tired of going she sent them, either to get her something she thought she wanted, or to get rid of them for a few minutes peace. Half the stuff they bought was chucked in the garbage or thrown into a corner; the other half was eaten and turned into fat.

Eventually Spider quit snaring rabbits. "Now I know how a rabbit feels," he explained to Archie. "I don't feel like killin' the little buggers anymore"; and he dedicated his Saturdays to sitting in the front room, watching his round offspring deepening and hardening the path connecting his front gate with the front door of the store. He became meditative. Sometime he thought of the path as a tightrope. He'd close his eyes and imagine his children like circus performers in fat tights, arms outstretched, balancing. If only they'd fall, he thought. But they always got over and always got back. And each time one of them got back he was, at first, less rich; but later on, more poor. His savings went. But because he and Archie put out such a prodigious pile of coal every week, he was able to pay for it all until Matthew was born. After Matthew it cost him more every week than he could earn. He sometimes thought of the picket fence around his house as a noose connected at the gate by a thick rope leading to the store. "If only a fella could cut that fuckin' rope."

He was behind a year's rent on his house and six months pay to the store when he saw the light late at night in the window of the store. He had been feeling sick for the first time in his life and for the first time, tired. He complained to his buddy, "Like the fella says, Arch, if a man can get the work, he could pay his bills. Now the pits don't even work every day."

"I know, Spider. 'Member the week we worked two weeks in one?"

"Even if we had the work. I'm after gettin' wore out. Don't think I could do that any more."

"Ah. She's pretty hopeless. I can't make it meself with five kids; and look how many you got."

"Ah. Well. If they had a lot of work. And a fella wouldn't be sick."

AS SOON AS HE SAW THE LIGHT, he rose from his chair in the front room. He opened the front door and walked out on his front step. He opened his gate calmly and stepped onto the short bridge which spanned the ditch in front of his house. As he crossed the little bridge over the ditch he felt dizzy. He stopped and looked down but the moonlight reflecting from the mixture of half melted snow and sewer water made his head spin worse and he had to close his eyes. He thought for a moment he was going to topple from the bridge into the sewer. But the dizziness went away. It was snowing a little. Thick flakes had whitened everything with a thin blanket except where they struck water in the ditches, but the path between the gate and the store could still be seen as an impression in the snow. He stepped off the bridge and onto the path and started across. When he opened his eyes he became dizzy again and he had to keep them closed. He opened them at a squint from time to time to make sure he was on the path. He spread his arms for balance. He felt like coughing but he held it back. He had the feeling that if he coughed he might faint.

Finally, he reached the step of the store. He put his fist through the glass and opened the lock from inside. He eased himself over the counter. He crouched down behind it and opened his eyes. There were three boxes of records: wholesale accounts, operating expenses, and customers' accounts. In the dark he couldn't tell them apart. He piled one box on top of another and hauled them to the back shop and chucked them into the raging fire.

He left the door open, walked down the steps onto the path and calmly, slowly, began to make his way back. The dizziness would not go away. He tried not to cough but his body demanded more air and when he took a deep breath the coughing dislodged gobs of greasy fluid from his lungs and he couldn't seem to clear them through his throat. When he tried to hurry he stumbled. He got to the end of the path but then he felt his head hit the bridge. Then suddenly things began to clear. His grandmother was smiling at him. "You rest on your tummy for a bit," she said. "I'll be back in a minute with some brown bread and black current jam and a nice hot cup of tea." That satisfied him and he dozed away.

The Glace Bay Miners' Museum

THE FIRST TIME I ever saw the bugger, I thought to myself, him as big as he is, me as small as I am, if he was astraddle on the road, naked, I could walk under him without a hair touching. That's the thought I had; he was coming down the aisle of the White Rose Café, looking to the right and looking to the left at the people in the booths. The size of him would kill you, so everybody was looking at him. I was looking at him too because I knew all the booths were full except mine. I was sitting in the last one, my back to the kitchen, so I could see everybody coming and going. He had a box in his hand, looked like a tool box, and I was wondering if he'd sit with me and show me what was in his box. I made a dollar keeping house for MacDonalds and came to the Bay to spend it on tea and chips and sit in the restaurant and watch the goings on. The going on was the same old thing: girls sitting with boys and boys sitting with girls, trying to pair off to suit themselves, and making a cup of tea and chips last as long as they could so they wouldn't have to leave. It was hard to find somebody on the street. You could go to the show and sit in the dark and hope somebody would sit next to you and hold your hand, but that cost money too, and hardly ever worked. It worked once for me, this fella sat beside me and I knew it was a chance because the theatre was almost empty. I figured he saw my hair before the lights went out. I had this lovely long hair. I was lucky enough, I bought a nut bar on the way in and I gave him a piece. He took my hand. He had a huge hand. Pan shovel hands we used to call people with hands like that. We used to think you got them from loading coal with a pan shovel. My hand disappeared in his in the dark. He put his big hand on top of my knees which I was keeping together. It felt like he had taken my hand off at the wrist and moved it up to my knee. I couldn't see it and for a minute I couldn't feel it and I was sitting there looking at his big mitt and wondering if my hand was still in it. Then it started to sweat and I could feel it again. We stayed like that through two shows. We never said a word. When we came out we walked down to Senator's Corner and down Commercial Street at Eaton's where the buses stopped. We never said a word. We stood next to each other and I stared at the Medical Hall and he stared at Thompson and Sutherland. Then the bus came for No. 11 and he got on. He didn't even look out the window at me.

I was sitting alone in the White Rose because none of the boys would sit with me and none of the girls would because the boys wouldn't. For one thing I had a runny nose. They called me names and if a boy went with me they called him names. George McNeil walked home with me from

school one day—it was on the way to his house anyway—
and I heard in the cloakroom the next day—they had a vent
between the boys' cloakroom and the girls'—I heard somebody from another class say to him—"I see you're taking
out snotface these days. Don't forget to kiss her on the back
of her head."

For another thing I screwed a couple of boys when I
was a little girl. I didn't know you weren't supposed to, but
I didn't want to anyway, and I wouldn't but this fella offered me a nickel and I never had a nickel. Then he asked if
I'd do it with his cousin and I said no. But then he came to
me himself, the cousin, and told me he went to the wash-
house every Saturday his father was on day shift for five
times and waited for him to come up and waited for him to
shower and followed him to the pay office and asked him
for a dime, and had to promise to cut enough sticks for the
week. I found out later he sold two quarts of blueberries
that he stole, but he wanted to tell me a nice long story.
Anyway I felt sorry for him, and he had fifty cents. So he
told me to meet him up in the woods by the Scotchtown
road between the bootleg pits and Rabbit Town. I didn't
know then that he didn't want to walk up there with me.
Anyway, I didn't really screw either one of them because
they didn't know how to do it and it was too late before I
could tell them, although, God knows, I knew little enough
myself of the little there is to know. They didn't walk home
with me either, neither one. But they told everybody I was a
whore. So I was not only a whore, but a snot-nosed whore.

You could hardly blame the boys and girls for not sitting with me.

So I was sitting alone in the last booth at the White Rose Café when this giant of a man with a box in his hand came bearing down the aisle looking left and right, and he kept on coming until he got to my booth and saw there was nobody there but me. I remember it seemed like it got darker when he stood in front of me, he blacked out so much light with the size of him. He had on a big lumberjack shirt. I thought, when he stood there holding his box, before he said anything, I said to myself, I wish he'd pick me up and put me in his shirt pocket.

"Can I put this here on your table?" he said; he pointed his chin at his box.

"Suit yourself," I said to him awful loud. He was so big, I thought I had to yell for him to hear me.

"Can I sit down, then?" he said.

"Suit yourself again," I said. So he put his box on the table and sat down opposite me, and I could feel his knees about an inch from mine. I could feel the heat coming from his knees. I could have exploded I was so happy. But I kept my lips tight.

The waitress pounced on us right away. "Hi snooker," she said. She was dying to find out who this fella was. So was everybody in the restaurant. I could see the ones facing me. I could feel the ones not facing me wishing they had sat on the other side of the booth. Nobody knew who he was. I just wanted to know what he had in the box.

"Something?" Kitten said, and looked at me and looked at him.

"I had something," I said.

"Would you have something else?" the man said. "I'd like to buy you a bite to eat if you don't mind." I near died. That was the first polite thing anybody ever said to me since my father got killed.

"I don't mind if I do," I said.

"Well, what is it then?" Kitten said. "What you want?"

"I'll have a cup of tea and an order of chips," I said.

"Will you now?" Kitten said.

"Yes," I said. "I will."

"I'll have the same," the man with the box said.

"Thank you," Kitten said, and wrote it down, saying very slowly to herself like she was talking to a baby: Two orders of chips and two orders of tea. "That will be fine," she said, looking at me and looking at him, "I'll go see if we got any."

She went away and I looked at my little hands and I could feel my knees getting warmer and warmer. I couldn't think of anything to say. My back was cold and I thought I might start to shake if I didn't talk, but I couldn't think of anything. I looked up at him and he was looking at his hands. He had a lot to look at. Nobody said a word till Kitten came back. "Here you are," she said, "two teas and two chips. Medium rare."

We ate a few chips and took the bags out of our teas and put them in the ash tray. Then he said: "Well, what do you think?"

"I think you're the biggest son of a bitch I ever saw," I said.

He looked at me then when I said that, as if I just came in and the look of him made me feel as if I just came in, I felt my back get warm, and I leant back against the back of the booth. He started to laugh. He must of laughed for two minutes but it seemed to me like two days, and it sounded like somebody playing some kind of instrument I never heard before. When he stopped, he said, "Know what I think?"

"What?" I said.

"I think you're the smallest son of a bitch I ever saw."

Then we both of us laughed for two minutes. Then we talked about the weather as if nothing happened, but I could feel the heat on my knees. After a while he said: "Well now. What's your name?"

"Margaret MacNeil."

"Well now, Miss MacNeil. It's been a pleasure meeting you. Do you come here often?"

"Every week at this same exact time," I said.

"Very well then," he said. "Perhaps we'll meet again. What do you think?"

"Suit yourself," I said.

"O.K.," he said, "I will. My name is Neil Currie." Then he got up and opened the box.

When he got the box open it was full of brown sticks and a plaid bag. Bagpipes! I never seen bagpipes before. Never knew there was any. Never heard them before. God only knows I heard them enough since. He pulled it all out of the box and started putting sticks on sticks till it was together; then he pumped it up. It snarled a couple of times, then when he had it between his arm and his ribs he came down on it with his elbow and it started to squeal, and everybody in the café either leaned out or stood up to look at the God-awful racket.

Then his fingers started jumping and it started playing something I don't know what it was. To me it sounded like a cut cat jumping from table to table and screaming like a tiger. Before you knew it the Chinaman came from the front. He didn't stop, he just slowed down to squeeze by the man and the pipes. When he got through he walked backwards a minute toward the kitchen and yelled: "Get that goddam fiddle out of here." Then two big Chinamen came out of the kitchen; I always thought Chinamen were small until I saw them two. They each had a hand of cards like they were playing cards and kept their hands so nobody could peek at them while they were out. They were just as big as Neil was, maybe bigger, and you never saw how fast two men can put one man and an armload of bagpipes out of a restaurant and into the street.

I went out after him. I took him out his box. I passed the Chinamen coming back in. They didn't do nothing to him, just fired him to the street and went back with their cards. He was sitting on the street. I helped him stuff his bagpipes in his box. Then he stood up and took the box in his hand. He looked down at me and he said, "One thing I thought a Chinaman would never have the nerve to do is to criticize another man's music. If I wasn't drunk, I'd give you my pipes to hold and I'd go back in there and get the shit kicked out of me."

"Where do you live?" I said.

"I have a room down on Brookside."

"Want me to walk down?"

"Where do you live?"

"I live in Reserve."

"Let's get the bus, then, I'll see you home. Sober me up. Perhaps you could make us a cup of tea."

"O.K.," I said.

"You live with your father and mother?"

"I live with my mother and grandfather. My father got killed in the pit. Come on. It's starting to rain. My brother too."

The rain banged on the roof of the bus all the way to Reserve and when we got off it was pouring and muddy all the way up to the shack where we lived. My father built it himself because, he said, he never would live in a company house. He had to work in the goddam company mine, but he didn't have to live in the goddamn company house, with god only knows who in the next half. My mother said he was too mean to pay rent, but only when he wasn't around did she say it. She only said it once to his face. But he got killed. They had a coffin they wouldn't even open it.

It was dark even though it was only after seven. It was October. We had to take off our shoes and ring out our socks from walking in puddles up the lane. We didn't have a real road in. Just a track where they came with groceries and coal. We hung them down the side of the skuttle and our jackets on the oven door. "I'll get you an old pair of daddy's pants soon's Mama gets out of the bedroom. You're the first one I ever saw could fit."

"You're right on time, Marg," Mama said. "I think I'll run up the Hall. Who you got here?"

"You'll get soaked."

"I know, but I better go. I might win the thousand."

"This is Neil Currie."

"Where'd you find him?"

"In the Bay."

"Are you from the Bay?"

"No. I just came."

"Where from?"

"St. Andrew's Channel."

"Never heard of that. You working in the pit?"

"I was. I started but I got fired."

"You look like you could shovel. Why'd they fire you?"

"I wouldn't talk English to the foreman."

"You an Eyetalian?"

"No."

"Well, I have to run or I'll be late. Don't forget your grandfather, Margie, I hit him about an hour ago so he's about ready."

"O.K., Mom. Hope you win it."

"Me too."

That was my mother's joke; about hitting my grandfather. Anytime a stranger was in she said it. He had something wrong with his lungs. Every hour or two he couldn't breathe and we'd have to pound him on the chest. So somebody had to be in the house every minute. When Mama left I got Neil the pants. "You might as well keep them," I said. "They won't fit nobody else ever comes around here." Then I went in to change my dress.

I expected to be a while because I wanted to fix myself up on my mother's make-up. It was her room, though I had to sleep in it, and she had a lot of stuff for make-up. My brother slept in the other room with my grandfather. We just had three. Where you come in was the kitchen and that's where you were if you weren't in the bedroom or in the cellar getting potatoes. But I didn't stay to fix up because I just got my dress half on when he started wailing on his bag and pipes.

I stuck my head out the door. "Are you out of your brain?" I yelled but he couldn't hear with the noise. So I got my dress all on and went out and put my hands over two of the holes the noise came out. They have three holes. He stopped. "My grandfather," I said, "you'll wake him up." I no sooner said it when the knock came. "There he is now," I said. "I'm sorry," he said, "I forgot your grandfather."

"It's O.K.," I said. "I think it must be time for his hit now anyway." I went in and I got the surprise of my life.

He could talk, my grandfather, but he didn't. It hurt him to talk after he came back from the hospital once with his lungs and he quit. I don't know if it got better or not because he never tried again; same as he quit walking after he got out of breath once from it. He took to writing notes. He had a scribbler and a pencil by him and he wrote what he wanted: "Thump me chest; dinner; beer; water; piss pot; did she win; did you pay the lite bill; then put on the lites; piece of bread; ask the priest to come; time to go now father; I have to get me thump. No, Ian'll do it." See, that's just one page. He had a whole stack of scribblers after a while. There're all here. We have them numbered.

So I went in, and I was after sitting him up in place to do his thump; you had to put him in a certain way. And he started to bang his long finger on the scribbler he had in his hand.

"Tell him to play."

"Well Christ in harness," I said, which is what my grandfather used to say when he talked and now I always said it to tease him. "Watch your tong," he wrote me one day. "Somebody got to say it now you're dumb," I said. "If I don't it won't get said."

"Do you want your thump?" I said and he wrote in his scribbler, "No, tell him to play." So I told Neil to play. "Isn't that lovely?" Neil said and laughed. And he played. It sounded to me like two happy hens fighting over a bean, and when he stopped and asked me if I knew what tune it was I told him what it sounded like to me and he laughed and laughed.

"Do you like the tune?"

"It's not too bad."

"Would you see if your grandfather liked it?" So I

went. And he was sound asleep with his scribbler in his hands on his belly. He wrote on it: "When he comes back ask him if he can play these." And he had a list I couldn't read. Here it is here in the scribbler:

> *Guma slan to na ferriv chy harish achune*
>
> *Va me nday Ben Doran*
>
> *Bodichin a Virun*
>
> *Falte go ferrin ar balech in eysgich*

I took the scribbler out and showed it to Neil and he said he would. "I'll have to practice a little."

"Play some more now," I asked him. "Play that one again."

"What one?"

"The one you put him to sleep with."

"'Mairi's Wedding.'"

"Yes."

"About the bean and the chickens."

"Yes."

So he played. I was getting interested in it. My foot started tapping and my knees which I had been holding together all night fell. As soon as he saw that, I was sitting on a chair against the wall, he came over and came down to kiss me. I put my two feet on his chest and pushed. I was hoping to fire him across the room but nothing happened. It kept him off, but he just stayed there with his chest on my feet looking up my leg and me with a hole in my underwear.

"WHAT'S THE MATTER with you?" he said.

I said, "Just because you play that thing, don't mean you can jump me." He ran his hand down my leg and nearly drove me nuts.

"Fuck off," I said. I thought that would shock him back but he just stayed there leaning against my sneakers. He tried to take my hand but I just put the two of them behind the chair.

"I won't jump you till we're married," he said.

"Married?" I said. "Who'd marry you? You're nothing but a goddamn Currie." Then he started laughing and moved back.

"And why wouldn't you marry a goddamn Currie?" he said.

"Because they just come in your house, play a few snarls on their pipes and they think you'll marry them for that."

"Well, well, well," he said. "I'll tell you what, I'll play for you every night till you're ready. And I'll make you a song of your own."

"What kind of song?"

"I don't know, we'll wait and see what I can make."

"Well, well, well," I said. "I want a song a person can sing so I'll be sure what it's saying."

"O.K., I'll make you two. One to sing and one to guess at."

"Good," I said. "If I like them, well, who knows what might happen."

"What would you like for the singing one?"

"I don't know."

"Well, what's the happiest thing in your life or the saddest?"

"They're both the same," I said. "My brother. Not the one living here now but my older brother, Charlie. We called him Charlie Dave, though Dave was my father's name. That was to tell him from the other Charlie Mac-Neils. There's quite a few around here. Charlie Pig, and Charlie Spider. And a lot more. Charlie Big Dan. I really liked Charlie Dave."

"What happened to him?"

"He got killed in the pit with my father."

"How old was he?"

"He was just sixteen. He used to fight for me. Wouldn't let anybody call me names."

"He mustn't have been in the pit very long?"

"Not even a year. He started working with my grandfather just before he had to quit for his lungs. Then he started with my father. Then he was killed. They were both killed. He was good in school too, but he got married so he had to work. They didn't even have a chance to have their baby."

"What happened to his wife?"

"Oh, she's still around. She's nice. She had her baby. A sweet baby. They live up in the Rows. In a company house. With her mother and her sister." I started to cry then so I made a cup of tea.

SO AFTER THAT he came back every night and it was

nothing but noise. My mother took to going out every night. When I told her he asked me to get married, she said: "That man will never live in a company house. You'll be moving out of one shack and into another."

"I can stand it," I said.

"You can stand it," she said. "You can stand it. And is he going to work?"

"He's going to look up at No. 10."

"Good," she said. "He can work with Ian. They can die together. And you can stand it. And you can live in your shack alone. Stand it, then."

The first night, after he played one of the songs my grandfather asked him, he played one he said he made for me. I loved it. It made me grin, so I kept my head down and I held my knees together with my arms.

"What's the name of it?" I asked.

"The name of it is 'Two Happy Beans Fighting Over A Chicken.'"

"Go whan," I said.

"Do you like it?"

"Not bad. What's the real name?"

"'Margaret's Wedding,'" he said.

"Christ in harness." I almost let go my knees.

The next night he played it again and he played another one for my grandfather. Then we went up the Haulage Road to No. 10 to get Ian. I always went to walk home with him because when he started he was scared when he was night shift to come home alone in the dark. I kept on ever since. Sometimes he had a girl friend would go. I never asked him if he stopped being scared. He never often had to try it alone. He didn't come home that night, he decided to work a double shift. So we walked back alone that night, but we took to going up together for Ian when he was night shift till Neil got the job there too and they were buddies in the pit so they worked the same shifts and came home together till we got married and moved to the Bay.

They fought like two mongrels. Miners said they never saw two men enjoy their work so much because it kept them close enough so they could fight every minute. Then on Sunday afternoon they came to our home and they sat in the kitchen and drank rum and played forty-five and fought and fought and fought.

What they fought about was politics and religion, or so they said. Ian would tell Neil that the only hope for the miner was to vote CCF and get a labour government.

"How are you going to manage that?"

"By voting. Organizing."

"When is that going to happen?"

"We have to work for it."

"The future?"

"Yes, the future."

"There's no future," Neil would say.

"There has to be a future."

"See in the bedroom, Ian. See your grandfather. That's the future."

"Well, he's there. The future is there."

"He's there all right. He can't breathe, he can't talk, he can't walk. You know the only thing he's got? Some old songs in his head, that he can hardly remember, that your father hardly even knew and you don't know at all. Came here and lost their tongues, their music, their songs. Everything but their shovels."

"Too bad you wouldn't lose yours. Have a drink and shut up."

"I will not shut up. However, I will have a drink."

He seemed so drunk to me I thought it'd spill out his mouth if he took more; but he took it. "Nothing left," he said. "Nothing. Only thing you can do different from a pit pony is drink rum and play forty-five."

Ian pointed to the cat curled up on the wood box. "Look, it's almost seven o'clock," he said. "Why don't you take that tom cat and go to Benediction since you like to sing so much. Then you can sing with him tonight. Out in the bushes. He goes out same time as you leave."

"What are you talking about?"

"You're buddies. You and the cat. You can sing near as good as he can. He's near fond of religion as you are."

"All I can say," Neil said, "is pit ponies can't go to church."

"Is that all you can say?" Ian said. "Well all I can say is, if a pit pony went to church, that would do him some lot of good."

"Ian, you do not understand what I am talking about."

"That is the God's truth for you, Neil. Now why don't you go on the couch and have a lay down."

And that's the way Sunday afternoon and evening went. We could've been out for a walk, just as easy, and more fun.

But that second night that he came we walked down the Haulage Road, pitch black, and he sang me the song I asked him for about my brother. He sang it over and over till I knew it by heart. He sang it to me. "That's lovely," I told him.

I took him by the arm behind his elbow and slowed him down till he stopped and turned. I was crying but I told him anyway. "I'm going to get married to you." We kissed each other. Salt water was all over our lips. I think he must have been crying too. I wrote the song down in one of my grandfather's scribblers when we got back. Here it is here in this one here.

> *My brother was a miner*
> *His name was Charlie David*
> *He spent his young life laughing*
> *And digging out his grave*
>
> > *Charlie Dave was big*
> > *Charlie Dave was strong*
> > *Charlie Dave was two feet wide*
> > *And almost six feet long.*
>
> *When Charlie David was sixteen*
> *He learned to chew and spit*
> *And went one day with Grandpa*

To work down in the pit.   (chorus)

When Charlie David was sixteen
He met his Maggie June
On day shift week they met at eight
On back shift week at noon.   (chorus)

When Charlie David was sixteen
He said to June "Let's wed"
Maggie June was so surprised
She fell right out of bed.   (chorus)

When Charlie David was sixteen
They had a little boy
Maggie June was not surprised
Charlie danced for joy.   (chorus)

When Charlie David was sixteen
The roof fell on his head
His laughing mouth is full of coal
Charlie Dave is dead.

The next night when he came I told him I had to pay him back for his songs. I'd tell him a story.

"O.K.," he said. "Tell me a story."

"This is a true story."

"That's the kind I like," he said.

"O.K. There was this fella worked in the pit, his name was George Stepenak, he was a Pole, they eat all kinds of stuff, took garlic in his can, used to stink. His can would stink and his breath would stink. The men used to tease him all the time, which made him cross. One day my father said:

"'George, what in the name of Jesus have you got in your can?'

"'Shit,' George said to my father.

"'I know that,' my father said. 'But what you put on it to make it smell so bad?'"

When my grandfather found out I told him a story to pay him back for the song, he wanted to tell him one. He wrote it out for him in a scribbler. Here it is here. Well, he didn't write it all out, he just wrote it out for me to tell it.

"Tell about Jonny and Angie loading in the 24, the roof so low they hadda take pancakes in their cans."

That's the way it went from then on. Every night he'd come and play and sing. Me and my grandfather would tell or write stories. My brother even would sing when he was on day shift or back shift. But he worked a lot of night shift. That's the way it went till Neil got work. When he got work we got married as soon as he built this house. Soon as he got the job he said, "I got some land on North Street. I'll build a house before we get married. It's right on the ocean. You can hear the waves." And he did. He did. And you can see, it's no shack. He must of been a carpenter. Soon as the house was finished, we got married and moved in. Him and my brother Ian were buddies by then, working the same shifts. They both got killed the same minute. I was up to Reserve keeping house for my mother when I heard the whistle. I heard the dogs howling for two nights before so soon's I heard the whistle I took off for the pit. They both just were taken up when I got there. They had them in a half ton truck with blankets over them.

"Take them to Mama's," I said.

"We got to take them to hospital."

"You take them to Mama's, Art. I'll wash them and I'll get them to the hospital."

"Listen, Snooker, the doctor's got to see them."

"I'll call the doctor."

"I can't."

"Listen, you bastard. Whose are they, yours or mine? You haven't even got an ambulance. I'll wash them, and wherever they go, they'll go clean and in a regular ambulance, not your goddamn half broken down truck."

So he took them down to Mama's and they carried them in and put one on Mama's bed and one on the couch in the kitchen. I knew what to get. I saw Charlie Dave keep a dead frog for two years when he was going to school. I went to the Medical Hall and got two gallons. Cost me a lot. I got back as fast as I could. I locked the house before I left so's nobody could get in. Mama was visiting her sister in Bras d'Or and I didn't know when she'd be back.

When I got back, there was a bunch around the door. They started to murmur.

"Fuck off," I said. "I'm busy."

To make matters worse, my grandfather was left alone all that time. He died. Choked. I took his lungs. It wasn't so much the lungs themselves, though, I think they were a good thing to take, though they don't keep too well, especially the condition he was in, as just something to remind me of the doctor who told him he couldn't get compensation because he was fit to work. Then I took Neil's lungs because I thought of them connected to his pipes and they show, compared to Grandfather's, what lungs should look like. I was surprised to find people have two lungs. I didn't know that before. Like Neil used to say, look and ye shall see. I took Neil's tongue since he always said he was the only one around still had one. I took his fingers too because he played his pipes with them. I didn't know what to take from Ian so I took his dick since he always said to Neil that was his substitute for religion to keep him from being a pit pony when he wasn't drinking rum or playing forty-five.

Then my mother came in. She went hysterical and out the door. I had each thing in its own pickle jar. I put them all in the tin suitcase with the scribblers and deck of cards wrapped in wax paper and the half empty quart of black death they left after last Sunday's drinking and arguing. I got on the bus and came home to the Bay and put in the pipes and Neil's missal and whatever pictures were around. Then I took the trunk to Marie, my friend next door, and asked her to put it in her attic till I asked for it. Don't tell anybody about it. Don't open it. Forget about it. Then I came back here and sat down and I thought of something my grandmother used to sing, "There's bread in the cupboard and meat on the shelf, and if you don't eat it, I'll eat it myself." I was hungry.

I knew they'd come and haul me off. So I packed my own suitcase, Neil's really, but mine now. They came with a police car and I didn't give them a chance to even get out of the car. I jumped right into the back seat like it was a taxi I was waiting for. I just sat right in and said, "Sydney River please." Sydney River, if you're not from around here, is the cookie jar where they put rotten tomatoes so they won't spoil in the barrel. So they put me in till they forgot about me; then when they remembered me they forgot what they put me in for. So they let me go.

My mother lived in the house all the time I was away. I told her to, to keep it for me and give her a better place to live. When I got back I told her: "You can stay here and live with me, Mother, if you like."

"Thanks, anyway," she said. "But I'm not feeling too good. I think I'll go back to Reserve."

"So stay. I'll look after you."

"Yes, you'll look after me. You'll look after me. And what if I drop dead during the night?"

"If you drop dead during the night, you're dead. Dead in Glace Bay is the same as dead in Reserve."

"Yes. And you'll look after me dead, too, I imagine. You'll look after me. What'll you do? Cut off my tits and put them in bottles?"

I said to her, "Mother, your tits don't mean a thing to me."

By then she had her suitcase packed and she left walking. "Have you got everything?" I called.

"If I left anything," she yelled back, "pickle it."

"O.K.," I said. She walked. Then she turned and

yelled, "Keep it for a souvenir."

"O.K.," I yelled.

I was sorry after that I said what I said. I wouldn't mind having one of her tits. After all, if it wasn't for them, we'd all die of thirst before we had our chance to get killed.

Marie came over then with the suitcase and we had a cup of tea and she helped me set things up. We had to make shelves for the jars. Everything else can go on tables and chairs or hang on the wall or from the ceiling as you can see. Marie is very artistic, she knows how to put things around. I'm the cook. We give tea and scones free to anyone who comes. You're the first. I guess not too many people know about it yet. A lot of things are not keeping as well as we would like, but it's better than nothing. Perhaps you could give us a copy of your tape when you get it done. That might make a nice item. It's hard to get real good things and you hate to fill up with junk just to have something.

Lauchie and Liza and Rory

I KNEW HE'D TAKE HER IN. I couldn't predict it, mind you, a minute before it happened, but when it did I said as a person often does: I knew it. Once it got to the point, he had to.

She wasn't even good looking. I can say that because she looked an awful lot like me. Red hair. Not the kind that glistens and goes good with green sweaters, but the other kind that looks like violin strings made of carrots. It had a part in the middle looked like an axe-cut, and it was pulled back hard and flat and tied at the back in a little ball you'd swear was nailed to the back of her neck. The same way I did it myself. She didn't exactly have buck teeth, but when her lips were closed her mouth was a little mound like she was keeping an orange peeling over her teeth. When she opened her mouth to talk you could see her teeth were round, and big, and almost the same color as her hair.

My brothers were identical twins, but as people they were day and night. Liza married Lauchie, the one everybody said was the good one. I could of told her, but I didn't. Even Mother, a smart woman, thought Rory would be a

113

gangster even after he went to work in the pit like everybody else. "He won't last," she said. "He'll get fired, if he don't get killed first, doing something foolish." One Friday in the winter he left with a quart of rum and a dozen beer and a smile and never showed up 'til a week from Monday, out of a taxi, a cast on one leg from toe to hip, a smile on his face, two crutches, and two poles, and one ski.

"You fool," I said when I got him in the house and sat him down on the sofa. "You can't ski."

"Whyn't you tell me that 'fore I left?" he said, and, of course, the big smile.

"The beginning of the end," my mother said, with her eyebrows.

Lauchie went steady with Liza six months. Then he took her home to meet me and Mother and Rory. Soon as she laid eyes on Rory she knew right then she made a mistake. How she knew I don't know. There wasn't a hair of difference between them. Rory knew it too. He shook hands with her. He never shook another person's hand in his life. He put out his big paw and she put her little red one in it, and he put his other hand on her shoulder; you could see her sink under it a fraction. You could almost see her eyes lock into his. "You'll like living here, Liza," he said. "It's a lot of fun if you look at it the right way."

"We'll not be living here," Lauchie said.

"Oh," said Rory. "I thought you were, next door, when the MacDonnells move out."

"Well, we are," Lauchie said. "The there is not here.

This is a duplex. Two different houses; one building."

"Some say it's a duplex," Rory said. "I say it's a company house."

"Well, what's the difference?"

"Difference is simple," Rory said. "In a duplex you can't here people drink water on the other side."

Lauchie wouldn't marry her 'til the MacDonnells moved out, so we had six months to watch her trying to make up her mind. Of course, she couldn't be sure Rory loved her. He might of been laughing at her. With him you couldn't tell for sure. I could, but I'd been watching him for years. Every time she came to the house he shook her hand, and he curled his middle finger so it stuck in her palm, but he did it so it looked like he was making fun of Lauchie, how formal he was when he introduced them. "Rory," he had said, "may I present to you my fiancée, Liza." And Rory shook her hand, like he did every time after, even after the marriage, and said, like an Englishman in the movies, "Awfully good of you to come," and everybody about doubled over laughing, except, of course, Lauchie and, of course, our mother; she stood there and waited for things to get back to "normal."

So Liza and Lauchie got married; Mother died—"mission accomplished, I suppose," Rory said. And they lived across the wall from us, and honest to God we never heard a peep out of them 'til their kid was born. Then we heard the kid. They called him Rory. He cried for two years.

When he stopped, Liza started. Both our stairs went up the wall that separated us and I first heard her through that wall, sitting on her stairs, sobbing. After that I took to going over every day to console her, but she never admitted to anything, though she knew I knew. She caught on pretty quick how much alike we were. She talked about it one night we were playing cards, which we did every Friday. "If me and her," she said, meaning me, "if we got our x-rays mixed up, they wouldn't be able to tell which one had T.B." We all looked at her but Lauchie; he looked at his cards.

"What's it mean, anyway, T.B.?" he said.

"Tough biscuit," Rory said.

"You wouldn't need an x-ray to figure that out," I said, thinking to make a joke, but when I looked at Liza for her little smile, she was crying, and I knew there was no secret between us.

When little Rory was five and about to go to school they left him with us on the miners' vacation and went to Halifax to visit Liza's sister and get Lauchie's lungs looked at. "The little bugger needs a little fun before he goes to school," Rory said, and gave him every minute of his time, took him everywhere, showed him everything he could think of, even took him down the pit and showed him where him and his father worked.

When Lauchie and Liza came back, the boy wouldn't go back with them. They had to drag him back. Then he started school and every day he came home he came to the wrong gate and landed in our place. Lauchie would have to

116

come over and drag him back.

"I thought I told you to come straight home."

"I forgot," he'd say.

He kept it up 'til we locked him out. We had to, to keep Lauchie from getting desperate. But he'd start again every time he went through a new phase of growing, until he got to be nine, and after that he wouldn't do his homework except at our place. He hated school, but he was first in his class because he did so much homework. Of course, Rory helped him; he couldn't resist; and when he got to Grade Nine and Rory couldn't help him anymore he started to teach big Rory. He taught him Algebra, French, Latin, Geometry, Chemistry, English, and God knows what all. He used to bring home the exams and Rory would do them and make high marks. "If I'd a known I was that smart I'd a stayed in school," he'd say. "Probably coulda been a teacher."

Of course he'd show off in the wash-house and turned it into a big joke. "What did you learn today, Rory?" somebody'd say.

"Today I learned that the sailor loves the girl," he'd say.

"And what have you got for homework?"

"For homework we have the girl loves the sailor, but I know it already, puellam nauta amat."

"What would that be in Gaelic?"

"In Gaelic, I couldn't say. I'm a Latin scholar. You'd have to ask me grandmother."

But he wouldn't carry it too far. He knew Lauchie felt bad and Rory wasn't a mean man, no matter how much he liked to make fun.

Once young Rory got to high school his home was nothing to him but bed and board. He had his tea first thing in the morning and last thing at night with us. He went into his side of the house for meals and bed. Nothing to do about it; he was too big then to make him. Liza sat on the stairs and sobbed. Rory felt bad but nothin' he could do, and he couldn't help it that he enjoyed the boy so much. I just watched. I knew something had to happen.

When it happened, it happened very quietly. Of course, that was Liza's way; but I was surprised; I expected a big fight; after all, seventeen years is a long time.

When young Rory graduated he got a big Knights of Columbus Scholarship and off he went to College. Liza picked the worst day she could find. It was coming down in buckets. She took her big suitcase and a kitchen chair and sat in the road between the two gates in her Burberry and big-rimmed felt hat. It was the first time she ever looked beautiful. It was a Sunday. Both men were home. She went out after Mass and Rory and Lauchie, each in his own side of the house, opened the front doors and watched through their screen doors as she sat there in the mud. In those days there was no pavement, or even a ditch; the road came right up to the picket fence and she sat at the edge of it between the two gates. Talk about a sight. I can still see Rory standing there, peering through the screen, cup and saucer in his hand, sipping tea. And Lauchie on the other side, the same. I knew he would be. I just went over to check.

"What do you think, Lauchie?" I asked him.

"I think it has to be up to him."

And so it was. About six o'clock, Rory said to me, "You better go and tell her to come in. She'll stay there all night."

So in she came. Put on dry clothes and sat and had tea. She cried. They were tears of joy. She was ashamed of them, but couldn't help it. "I realize," she said, "that I'm probably not making anybody happy but myself. I can't help it."

After a few days when we all got the feeling it was set-tled for good, I moved over with Lauchie.

"Are you mad, Lauchie?" I asked him.

"Nobody to be mad at," he said. "I'd like to be mad. But, you know, it's not Rory's fault. He didn't encourage her; you know that. Just the opposite. Same for Liza. She tried for seventeen years. It's not my fault. It's nobody's fault. Unless it's all our faults. It should of been fixed up seventeen years ago when it started wrong. We all knew."

I certainly didn't know he knew.

"Well," I said, "young Rory will be surprised when he comes home for Christmas."

"I wonder," Lauchie said. "He's supposed to be smart, too. I don't imagine college'll take it out of him that quick."

Dies Irae

WHILE HER FRIEND AND FAVOURITE patient Joce-
lyn AuCoin sucked from her machine in brief gasps the last
cubic litres of oxygen her cancerous lung would ever enjoy,
Marie, in the hall, breathed easily, in spite of a two-flight
stair climb; her pulse was a healthy 85 and would soon
drop, if she sat down, to 65, and she watched herself put
one foot in front of the other, saying to herself: this is the
way one walks, putting one foot in front of the other, in
more or less a straight line, absolutely incredible, as Jocelyn
might say, if Jocelyn could put one foot in front of the other. I am not bored, she thought; things are a bit lousy, but
not boring, a bit stupid, but interesting, a bit trivial but
overwhelming Jocelyn but so what. Here I am walking
down the corridor of the hospital on my day off, in my
crumpled trench coat approaching a corner where I will almost certainly turn right.

At the corner she heard her name. She turned and saw
Dr. Ira N. Deedy smiling at her from a doorway.

"Marie," he said, "could you step in here a moment?"

"Of course, sir," Marie said. "What can I do for you
sir?" Her sarcasm was wasted. He held out a handful of
papers.

"These documents," said Dr. Deedy, "would you take them to the receptionist at the main door. She promised to type them, I need them this afternoon."

Marie kept her hands by her sides. She looked into Dr. Deedy's eyes until he was forced to look down at the papers he was holding in his hand. He seemed unable to decide whether he should return the papers to the table or ask Marie what was the matter. Finally Marie snatched the papers from his hand and clattered off down the hall and down two flights of stairs. She was back in three minutes. Deedy was still standing, astonished, in the doorway. She puffed and gasped and waved a piece of paper. She pushed Deedy ahead of her into the room, and sat him down behind the table.

"This is your receipt," she said as she gasped for air. "It certifies that I delivered your documents to Miss T.Y. Pest. Now would there be anything else?"

"No thanks, Marie, that's all."

"How about a nice cup of tea," she said, breathing hard.

"No thanks," he said.

"How about a peek up my skirt?"

Dr. Deedy, in reply, put his hands on the table, closed them to make a tight double fist, and stared at his knuckles until Marie left.

JOCELYN LAY ON HER BACK; her hair was black, in braids, her face was white and wasted; her lower lip, once full and sensual, was almost gone, and the thin line that was left of it clung to her teeth; her eyes, staring at a picture of a boat on the wall across from her bed, were open, stark, dead. Her hands, folded over her belly, held a page of white paper. Marie took it from her and sat in the chair at the foot of the bed and read it.

Dear Marie:

How in the hell are you, as we always said to each other, but this is for the last time. By the time you get this you might truthfully be able to say it of me. When you think of me, as I hope you will, once in a while, you can say to yourself I wonder how in the hell she is. Think of all the fun we had, Marie, think of all the fun we had.

Can you tell how calm I am. It's because I can die any time I want to now. I just have to let go. It gives me the feeling of control. But I know it's not going to last and I'll soon have to die whether I agree to it or not. It's early in the morning and it's your day off so I know you won't be here for a while. I have to talk to you now in case I can't when you come.

Thank you for being such a good friend and for waking me up, and for the fun we had. The times we were together were the times I was alive, the same as I was when I was a little girl on vacation, fishing with my grandfather. Just think, we both came from the same place and had to meet in Halifax.

I'm looking at the picture of my grandfather in his boat. I have the feeling he's waiting for me. It's a great comfort. It's the picture that most looks like him so I had it enlarged and framed. I want you to have it so make sure you get it. Take it now. I imagine myself stepping out of bed and into the boat and off we go. We'll both come back for you when the time comes. Please leave the picture to whoever you love the most.

Too bad we never got the chance to visit Cheticamp. Visit our roots, as they say. But they say there's nothing there anyway. My sister was back years ago. It's all part of the park. Superpark they call it. Imagine. I know you know this, but it's funny we never talked about it. Too busy, I guess, trying to convert the world. It's a thing that should be talked about. It's up to you. It's....

I had to stop. It's later now. I hear you talking to Deedy. It's been nice talking to you.

Au Revoir.

Jocelyn

P.S. Give something for me to Lynn, whatever you think. Keep everything that fits you and get rid of the rest. SAG.

MARIE REACHED OVER HER SHOULDER and took down the picture. Jocelyn looked like her grandfather. The eyes were the same. She closed them and sat down to read the letter again. Dr. Deedy came in, squeezed behind the chair, crossed the room and sat by the window.

"How's the patient?" he asked.

"She's fine now," Marie said. "She won't be a patient much longer."

"Well, that's encouraging."

"Yes."

"Are you writing a letter?"

"Reading one."

"From home?"

"Something like that."

"Not very newsy, I take it."

"How'd you mean?"

"Well, Jocelyn certainly seems to have lost interest in it, and you seem a bit flat yourself. You were quite lively a few minutes ago."

"Well, you're right, there's nothing new in it."

"Could I have a word with you in private?"

"Sure, go ahead."

"Couldn't we go to my office?"

"I have to meet somebody here so I can't leave, but we can talk here."

"Well...," Deedy said, and looked toward the bed.

"She won't hear," Marie said, smiling. "She's dead to the world."

"Well. I.... Since a while now.... You two.... Let me start again.... I'd like to apologize."

"What for?"

"For my behaviour."

"Don't even think about it."

"Let me explain first that I didn't come in here to apologize."

"Oh."

"In fact I came in to give you, and your friend here, but you, especially, a piece of my mind."

"Oh. What for?"

"Well, I was going to say that it's funny that you two think you're such shit hot nurses, and still you always have half a dozen people in the hospital mad at you at any one time."

"Well, I guess you said it after all."

"No, I didn't say it. When I was about to say it, it hit me. It just hit me that the fact is you two are shit hot."

"Thank you, Doctor, on behalf of me and my friend."

"I'm glad she's here. Even though she's not awake, maybe she's taking it in."

"I'm sure she is."

"It just hit me, you see, that you two could be counted on to do a first-rate job about ten percent of the time. The rest of what you did was a disaster."

"Oh yeah?"

"What hit me was that when you were doing what nurses should do, nursing, you were great, and that—do you mind me saying this?"

"Well, it seems once you get started there's no stopping you, is there?"

"I'm sorry.... I.... "

"No, no, no. Keep on telling me how wonderful I am, we are, I thought nobody noticed. I thought...." A knock on the door stopped the conversation.

"Am I interrupting something?"

"Ian, come in." She embraced him and introduced him. "This is Ira Deedy."

"Hello." Ian nodded.

"He was just telling me and Jocelyn what great nurses we are. You'll have to wait quite a while to meet her, I'm afraid."

"I'll be off," Deedy said, and left.

"Good-bye."

"Nice to meet you."

"Same."

"Like I said on the phone, Ian, it's my day off. It's a gorgeous day. Let's do something."

"What?"

"Oh well, let's walk till we think of something."

"O.K., let's go. I've never been in Halifax so it's up to you."

THEY WALKED ALONG Lower Water Street and up, they walked along Hollis and up, Barrington and up, Argyle and up; they talked about the past. They laughed a lot. They talked about their former careers in the grocery business.

"I got your number, mister man, when you tried to seduce me in the back shop of the co-op."

"I did not. I liked you, that's all."

"Sure you liked me. You had a growing problem. And I was handy."

"I did like you though."

"Oh, yes, I knew that. I could tell that when I noticed that instead of dressing up and coming with flowers and win-ing and dining me like some smooth guy might try to pull off, you just tried to lay me on a bag of oats in your overalls."

"Well, I was only young."

"You were old enough. We were both young, and old enough. What I felt bad about was the poor priest standing there bawling his eyes out. I'll never get over that."

"I don't think he even saw us."

"You don't?"

"I think he forgot where he was. He used to do that. He'd come to and he wouldn't know where he was or how he got there."

"I'll never forget that day. His face looked like a mask of melting wax."

"Yeah."

"And then we played cards as if nothing happened. This is Citadel Hill."

"Yes, I remember."

"You said you were never here."

"I remember from the book, *Barometer Rising*. The explosion must of been right out there."

"When did it happen?"

"I think it was 1917. Neil came back from the war in France and walked up here just like we just did. And looked out over the harbour a few days before it happened."

"What was it exploded?"

"A munitions ship. Funny, how I remember that. Even the name, *Mont Blanc*. It and a British cruiser collided and, boom."

"Many killed?"

"I don't know how many. Must of been thousands. This hill here saved a lot because it deflected the wind. I think everything below here was shot to hell."

"Too bad we don't have a beer and a bite to eat," Marie said, and sat on a spot of rich green grass.

"Yeah, too bad. Maybe later."

"Have a seat anyway, Ian. What about the hero?"

"In the book?" Ian said and sat.

"Yeah. Was he killed?"

"No, he wasn't killed. No, he and his girl and their daughter lucked out. Started a new life and all that."

"A little bit corny."

"No. I don't think so. It seemed O.K. at the time. Girl was a lot like you."

"How'd you mean?"

"Oh, tough. Smart. Beautiful. Bitchy."

"God, Ian, don't do that to me."

"What. I didn't say nothing much."

"Well it's not what you said, god-dammit; if you had used your mouth instead of your hand in the back shop, you'd of been like your friend in the book with a girl-friend and a baby to look after." Ian looked at her slyly and took her hand. "Thank Christ I'm old enough to know better now," she said.

"Know what?"

"To know your tongue doesn't mean it any more than your hand."

"How d'you know that?"

"Ian, don't make me laugh. Why'd you come to Halifax, anyway, Ian? And don't tell me you came to see me."

"Well, I had a good reason to come—but when I heard you were here, I came anyway."

"There you go again."

"C'mon," he said. "We'll walk up Quinpool, I'll show you."

"O.K.," she said. "For someone who's never been here before, you sure seem to know your way around."

ON THE WAY UP Quinpool Road they bought a quart of wine instead of beer because it would be easier to carry and disguise. They sat in the recessed doorway of a "bookstore," surrounded by bundles of *Playboy* magazines, delivered, but not yet taken inside.

"It is fitting, indeed, and just, no doubt," he said, "looking at the magazine covers, to be sucking on a bottle in a bag, like winos, surrounded by artificial faces, plastic teeth smiling, and reconstructed tits and renovated arses, imported from New York and California to assuage my loneliness while my dream is about to crumble before my very eyes."

"My goodness, Ian, could you be that drunk on a few slugs of wine?"

"I am drunk with disappointment. Contemplating disappointment."

"Holy Mary Mother of God!" Marie said. "You are drunk. But I must say, it suits you better than sober."

"What d'you mean, girl?" he said, and raised the bottle in the wrinkled bag in a sort of salute.

"I mean," she said, "in the first place, winos don't sit to drink Chateau Neuf du Pape from bottles in or out of bags. In the second place, it sounds like fun, but what the hell are you talking about?"

"It's no great fun, Marie, but laugh anyway."

"O.K., but what at?"

"Well. Let me put it another way. It is ironic, indeed, if not fitting, or just, that we should sit here among this debris, sucking Chateau Neuf du Pape from an old bag, while across this very street, behind the ancient fence, the Chateau of the Pope is about to be hit with a ball, and to crumble into rubble."

THE BUILDING across the street was made of brick. The windows had been taken out. The roof had been removed. It started to rain. Up to now Marie had noticed neither the building nor the weather. The tires rolling up and down Quinpool Road began to hiss. The crane operator climbed up the ladder to the cab, got in, pushed a lever and a huge ball came rising out of the ground but soon stopped. The crane operator stood up from his seat, searched his pockets, sat down again, pulled a lever and the huge ball descended. He got out of his cab and started walking around kicking debris as he went.

"Saved, for the moment," Ian said. Marie looked at him with a puzzled smile.

"That's the seminary," she said.

"Right."

"What's it got to do with you?"

"I came down to go to it."

"To be a priest!"

"Yeah."

"Why?"

"I thought it'd be a good thing to do. You're surprised."

"No, I guess not. Not when I think about it. Are you sure you want to?"

"No. But I don't think they should tear it down until I am," he said and laughed.

"Well, for Christ's sake," she said, "let's put a stop to it." She got up and went into the bookstore. Ian took a swig.

When she came out, she carried a clipboard with several pages clipped to it. On the top half of the first page she had written a variety of unintelligible scrawls and the address of the seminary. Pinned to the lapel of her trench coat a plastic card declared in large blue letters:

HALIFAX HISTORICAL SOCIETY

"C'mon dummy," she said. "I'll show you how to do this."

The crane operator watched their approach from behind his eyebrows, his head lowered. As they passed the crane, he looked up for a second, then bent his head again and kicked a shingle. He put one hand in a pocket.

"On second thought," she said to Ian, "you better stay with me till we settle this one."

"What about MacKenzie?" Ian said.

"Never mind that son of whore, he knows, he touches a brick, he'll be in court in the morning. Are you in charge here?"

"Jes drive the crane."

"Could I have your name please?"

"Danny MacIntyre."

"Well, Mr. MacIntyre, you've got quite a mess here."

"I jes got here."

"Well, what do you propose to do here?"

"Sent me down to knock her over."

"Do you realize we have a court injunction prohibiting any interference with this property? This is one of the oldest buildings in the city."

"Suits me," the man said. "I got the flu anyway. Just as soon be home in bed. Lost my watch in this junk. Let me lift the ball here a minute, eh. You look under see if it's there. Only place I never looked," he said climbing the ladder.

WHEN HE LIFTED THE BALL, Ian retrieved what was left of the watch; the crystal and hands were gone.

"Pretty well shot, ain't she," the man said. "Good strap though. She was gettin' pretty old anyway." He went to his car, got in and hissed off down the street.

Later, when they sat to eat, still living on the edge of

their bottle of Chateau Neuf du Pape, they were pleased with themselves, a delicate, fragile pleasure. They had come into the restaurant holding hands, conscious of how corny they appeared, her in her crinkled trench coat, himself in a worn suit, looking like Ingrid and Humphrey in Casablanca.

So touching they appeared that when they stood in the vestibule and looked down the long aisle of the restaurant, the host, astonished, rushed to them, his soutane flopping at his legs.

"Would you terribly mind," he said, "standing here a moment."

"Sure," Ian said.

"Don't move," he said, and rushed back to the end of the aisle, through a curtain of black lace into a pantry where the silverware and such stuff was kept. He reappeared with a camera and snapped at them several times from various angles and distances.

"THANK YOU," he said. "I'm a bird watcher by avocation, but I like to shoot unusual people too."

"Could we eat here?" Ian said.

"Of course, bien sur," he said and, still infected by their charm and his own, he stepped between them, when they let go each other's hand, and put his arms around their shoulders. "My name is Frankie," he said, "may I ask yours, we're not of your persuasion, here, but we're ecumenical."

"Humphrey," Ian said.

"Ingrid," Marie said.

"Goodness," he said, "we'd better sit you down, you'll miss your plane if you don't hurry."

He sat them by the window overlooking the harbour. A boat full of sails went by.

"That must be the *Bluenose*," Marie said. "Doesn't it make you feel like the nineteenth century? Or is it the eighteenth?"

"Hard to know what century to feel like," Ian said. "What is this place anyway, Marie, you been here before?"

"I thought you might find it just, indeed, and fitting. Can't you guess what's going on?"

"Well, it's awful churchy. That guy was wearing a soutane. Look! Over there, he's coming back with, what did they call that thing. A surplice?" And indeed it was, cut short, with short wide sleeves and trimmed with starched lace at the ends of the sleeves and bottom of the tunic. The wall opposite their table behind Ian was decorated with stained glass windows from floor to ceiling with lights turned on behind them to illuminate the words and figures represented on the glass. The windows had been composed of rectangular panes of glass arranged in sequence, but, apparently, the panes had been taken out, for cleaning perhaps or moving, and were put back in by someone who had never known, or had forgotten, or did not care about the proper sequence. Consequently, it came to pass that when St. John the Baptist was beheaded, St. Catherine's head rolled on the grass. John's head, however, turned up on St.

Clare, with St. Francis of Assisi behind it giving it a hair cut, so that he/she could take the veil. Later she gets her own head back in time to pray against the Saracens. Various historical and biographical revisions were explicit, but the chief value of the confusion lay in the fact that a canny spectator could design his own arrangement and bend history and biography to suit his will or his whim.

"HI," THE HOST SAID, "would you like to wear these? You don't have to, of course, but some people enjoy getting into the spirit of the thing."

"What is it?" Ian said.

"It's the stole."

"Stole."

"Let's try it, Ian," Marie said, "why not?"

"Why not?" Ian said, still in a good mood. "Why in hell not?"

"Good," said the host. He placed around their necks a long rectangular piece of linen. The ends of it came down in folds on their laps. "It's the old type," he said. "We had them made. We use them in place of a napkin which is what they were originally, in ancient Rome, you know. It's a bit like both a bib and a napkin. Would you like a complimentary litre of house wine, it's called Salvation Now, or would you prefer a mixed drink? We have all the regular drinks, plus several from our special liturgical list; the Mortal Sin is a popular favourite, but I could bring you our list."

"I think we'll stick with the wine," Ian said.

"Fine, fine. Perhaps you'll feel like a mortal sin later in the evening."

"It's not that we don't feel like it," Marie said, "it's just that this hardly seems the place...."

"I thought they did away with mortal sins," Ian said.

"Not at all," said the host, "they changed the name. Now it's called antisocial behaviour. You could hardly call a drink that. Anyway, here's your menu. I'll go fetch your wine." Ian looked at his menu. On the front was printed, "Loaves and Fishes, the menu according to Luke." He turned it over but the back was blank.

"I THOUGHT YOU'D have an explanation of your decor here," he said to the waiter, stopping him as he moved off.

"Oh, it's all explained on the altar stones," he said, "that's what we call our place mats, but let me tell you; what happened was," he said softly, "they decided to tear down the seminary, you know, and we decided, well what a bargain; it was junk to them; they were going to chuck the lot, so we spent a day with a truck, they were glad to get rid of it, you know, didn't charge us a red cent, so we got off with just the rent for the truck. We had a restaurant at the time called 'The Catacombs,' but it was just the name, we didn't have a decor, so this place was for sale, we bought it and moved in all our stuff. We consider we've really come up in the world. You have to have an interesting decor to survive in Halifax these days."

"Where's the crucifix?" Ian asked.

"Pardon."

"They must have had a crucifix in the chapel at the seminary."

"Oh, they did. It's in the catacombs; we call our basement the catacombs now, although it was another basement we had the restaurant in."

"Why don't you bring it up here?"

"Well, we thought about that. In fact we had a big meeting over it. And, well, first of all it was a huge thing with this big Jesus Christ on it, and well, there was nothing nice about it at all, you know, if it had been one of those Renaissance things, well maybe, but blood all over the legs, and hair matted with blood, and this awful grimace on his face, well, all in all, we decided we could do without it so we put it in the catacombs with the wine. We didn't want to go too far either, that was another point, even today, you know, there's such a thing as blasphemy."

"Any lobster?" Ian asked.

"Pardon."

"On the menu. If there's lobster that's what I'll have, without looking."

"I'm sorry. The only rule we have to do with food, to fit our decor, you know, is that we don't serve lobster till Quinquagesima Sunday. Then you can get it all through Lent; and on Ember Days, but this is not an Ember Day. We have every other kind of fish though. I'll go and get you your wine."

"Well?" Marie said, her chin in her hand, her lips pursed in a half smile.

"Well what?"

"Well, what d'you think of the 'Loaves and Fishes'?"

"If we're gonna have a nice time, I think I'll wait to answer till I have a sip of wine, my blood misses the Chateau Neuf du Pape."

THE HOST CAME BACK and in his train he led two surpliced teenagers with pimples and the wine and two silver chalices. Frankie put the place mats down.

"The boys will take your orders," he said. "If you're having fish I recommend the 'Baked Sole à la Beelzebub.'"

"Good," Ian said. "I'll have that."

"Me too," Marie said.

"O.K., boys. Thank you. How do you like the wine?"

"It's very nice," Ian said, "meek, but with a hint of inner strength."

"Yes, very good. It's Christian Brothers, of course. A little expensive for a house wine, but, well, in this house, what else could you have?"

"Perhaps Blue Nun," Ian suggested, "maybe you could hire a real one to serve it."

"What a marvellous idea! We have the wine, of course. Well, you know, we could dress up one of our slight and slender boys to do the serving; marvellous idea. My, my, my, yes. I'll bring you another complimentary litre for that idea. If you think of something else...."

"I will," Ian said.

"Frankie," Marie said, "why are we the only customers? When I was here before it was crowded."

"Oh, you know, you're early. This is choir night. Most of our regulars come tonight, but a bit later, so they can eat and enjoy the floor show. Enjoy your meal. If you need anything, just give me a tingle. I see the crowd is starting to come now, so you won't be lonely."

"Well," Marie said, when finally the meal and the wine were on the table between them, "alone at last, together, and burgundy already coursing through the veins, so what do you think?"

"I don't know whether to laugh or cry," he said.

"I think I'll likely do both."

"I'm surprised they didn't serve the bread as communion wafers."

"Yes, and it could be worse, Ian, Frankie might come out to consecrate the bread and wine."

"Frankie might think that would be going too far. Blasphemy, you know, my dear, does not undercut decor."

"Are you serious about the seminary?"

"I don't know any more. There's none here now, anyway. Maybe I'll go to Quebec. They must have one there. Though I wonder if it makes any sense any more. It was such a strong idea in my head I have the feeling I should follow it up. Oh God, let's not bother with it now, it gives me the shivers to talk about it in a place like this."

"I kind of like this place."

"Why?"

"Well, it's the only restaurant in town where you can

touch knees without having to slide down in your chair."

"My God, you're bad, Marie."

"It's not me, Ian. It's the Christian Brothers made me say it."

"I think it was a very sensible thing to say. I propose a toast to our knees, but only because the Christian Brothers insist."

"Our knees." Clink.

"You know, Ian, I don't think you're all that priesty."

"It's not a matter of being priesty. It's just a question of doing something worth doing. What d'you mean priesty?"

"Well, you don't seem that holy."

"How do I seem?"

"Well, there is a word for it. Something like holy, but even the Christian Brothers can't make me say it."

"Why not?"

"It doesn't go with my decor, I guess."

"But does it go with your heart?"

"Oh yes. Especially when I have my Christian Brothers with me, and you, of course. You know, we never toasted to our success."

"What success?"

"God, you have a poor memory. Don't you remember a couple of hours ago we confronted the men and machines that tear down the past to put supermarkets in its place. And we won."

"Oh yes, the capitalist dog. He put his tail between his

tires and slunk off. But, don't forget, tomorrow there will be more dogs in the yard; and will we be there to fight?"

"No. But we fought the right fight. You always lose in the long run. Right. Too bad we couldn't win for ten years, but to win for a day, that's not too bad."

"You're right. Here's to it. A short-lived but grand success." Clink.

"Here comes the band," Marie said, "I wonder what happened to the choir, or do choirs sing with bands?"

A DRUMMER took his place behind the altar rail and began to swish with his brushes, soft. He wore the brown habit of a monk with the hood bunched back at the neck. Another man in the same dress came and sat at the organ, and another with a clarinet sat on the altar rail and they began to play notes from random tunes. The room was nearly half full now and a comfortable murmur could be heard under the music.

"That's a nice sound, Ian."

"Yeah. What about the choir, I wonder." As he spoke four young men entered wearing the same garb as the band, but white hoods rather than brown covered their heads. Several people began to clap as the men filed behind the rail and stood in line in front of the stained glass windows.

The clarinet player picked up a microphone and said, "Good evening, ladies and gentlemen. Tonight, as you know, is choir night; and, of course we have with us the ever popular 'Castrati.' For those of you who are new patrons, I would like to tell you that if you look on the back of your altar stones you will find information about our first tune which has pretty well become our unofficial theme. Also there are the first few verses in Latin and a translation by one of our boys. The music itself is authentic, copied directly from the book you are told about there on the placemat."

IAN TWISTED in his chair to see the clarinet player make his speech; then he turned back, and as the band played an introduction, and the choir moved to the front, he read on the placemat that "authentic music and lyrics were all taken from the Paroissien Romain, contenant Le Messe et l'Office pour les Dimanches et les Fêtes, Chant Grégorian Extrait de l'Edition Vaticane et Signes Rythmiques des Bénédictines de Solesmes," and that all translations were by members of the choir. This note was followed by several verses of the "Dies Irae":

Messes des Morts

Séq. 1.

DI- es írae, dí-es ílla,   Sólvet saéclum in favílla :

Téste Dávid cum Sibýlla.   Quántus trémor est futúrus,

Quando jú-dex est ventúrus,   Cúncta stricte discussúrus!

Túba mí-rum spár-gens sónum   Per sepúlcra regi-ónum,

Cóget ómnes   ante thrónum. Mors stupé-bit   et natú-

ra,   Cum resúrget cre-a-túra,   Judi-cán-ti   responsúra.

Líber scríptus pro-fe-ré-tur,   In quo tó-tum continé-tur,

Unde múndus judi-cé-tur.   Júdex ergo cum sedébit,

Quídquid lá-tet apparébit :   Nil inúltum remanébit.

The song was followed by the note: "This is part of the Sequence of the Dead Mass and the first few lines are translated thus: The day of wrath, the day of dread,/ The day that Sibyl and David said/ Would be the day beyond the dead." By the time he finished reading, the choir had finished several verses, singing the English first and then the Latin. Ian looked up in time to see a large tear drop from Marie's cheek into her wine. It was followed by another. Her eyes were shining with them.

"MARIE, what's the matter? Is it the music?"

"Yes. It's the music. It's so beautiful. And Jocelyn is dead."

"We just left her a few hours ago."

"She was dead when we were there. I just couldn't bear to tell anybody until I got used to it."

"Are you used to it now?'

"Well, I'm holding it at arm's length. The music got to me for a minute there. It was our favourite tune."

"It's a funny favourite tune for two nurses."

"Oh, we weren't nurses to start with. We were nuns together."

"You were a nun?"

"Well, you know I always figured after I got all my sisters and brothers through nursing school, and secretarial school and technical school and this school and that school, well, I'd just get married to you."

"You should have told me."

"Well, Ian, you were long gone. And anybody half decent was long gone too, or had two kids already. So I hemmed and hawed a while and finally entered the convent. 'See you in a week,' my mother said. She would have been right, too, except I met Jocelyn. Separate we were in the wrong place but together we stuck it out for quite a while."

"What happened?"

"Oh, we'd likely still be there if they'd let us be nurses. We thought of ourselves as Florence Nightingales but they told us to be teachers. We went. We studied theology and philosophy and every other kind of thing and then we were teachers and spent our time peeling ski pants and overshoes off cute kids. We stood it quite a while but then that was it for the both of us. Jocelyn said, you know, Marie, this is kinda comical but who wants to spend a whole life as a clown. So when they wouldn't let us change to nursing we turned in our heads and flew the coop."

"And went into nursing."

"And went into nursing. And we were just getting ready to chuck that when Jocelyn got sick."

"You didn't like nursing either?"

"Oh, we liked nursing. But we didn't get a chance to do much. It was the same thing all over. How much philosophy do you need to get off an overshoe. Like Jocelyn said, you know Marie this is kinda comical and these doctors are cute, but who wants to spend a whole life as a flunky. But then she got sick. We had quite the careers and we had a lot of fun, and we loved that song and we loved the Mass of the Dead that it's in, but all that stuff is long gone. And here we are, a former nun and would-be priest and Jocelyn is dead and nobody but me to put her in the ground."

"What'll we do, then? Would you like to go back to the hospital?"

"I've been trying to think what Jocelyn would want."

"And what would she want?"

"Jocelyn would say, 'Don't sit there like a goddam fool, get a nice bottle of wine, and you and your friend go to our apartment and celebrate the reunion of me and my grandfather.'"

"Have you any wine where you live?"

"No," Marie said. Her nose was running now. "But

you leave that to me, I know how to get it." She sobbed and sniffed and her eyes shone. "Ian, I don't know if I'm crying or laughing."

WHEN THE CHOIR FINISHED the "Dies Irae" Ian requested "Pange Linqua" and delighted the choir, one of whom said, astonished, "You're quite conversant with the liturgy, I take it," for which Ian could concoct no suitable reply so he sat down with Marie and listened:

> *Pange Linqua gloriosi*
> *Corporis mysterium*
> *Sanguinisque pretiosi*
> *Quem in Mundi pretium*
> *Fructus ventris generosi*
> *Rex effudit Gentium*

When they had finished Marie sent a note. The clarinet player took it and spoke into the microphone, "We have a request for Psalm 129, dedicated to Jocelyn who could not be here tonight in the flesh but who is here in spirit." The band played an introduction and stopped; then the choir chanted the words: *De profundis clamo ad te, Domine, Domine, audi vocem mean.....*

WHEN THE CHOIR FINISHED, Ian and Marie pooled some money to pay the bill. "Let me look after the tip," Marie said. She took a fist full of bills from her bag, wrote a note and stuffed it with the bills in an envelope and sealed it. She called Frankie and explained to him that the tip was inside the fat envelope, along with instruction on how to divide it. He held out his hand, but she offered him only the bill and enough money to pay for it.

"WE'D LIKE TO SEE the crucifix," she said.

"Pardon?"

"We'd like to see the crucifix."

"It's in the basement," Frankie said dubiously.

"O.K. Let's go," she said, "we'll put our coats on so we won't catch cold."

FOR A WHILE, the Christ could not be found. The cellar was large and it was a maze of randomly placed wine shelves; finally, however, they discovered it near a stair, behind a pile of junk, the penitent side of a confessional, a wooden altar coming apart at its seams, and assorted candelabra, sacramentals and ecclesiastical paraphernalia. It was upside down, the top stick had broken off and the crown of thorns was embedded in the dirt cellar floor. Frankie and Ian pulled it out and examined it. In the meantime, Marie selected two Chateau Neuf du Pape and two Christian Brothers burgundy.

"DO YOU WANT TO BUY IT?" Frankie said. "Is it an antique?"

"It might be," Ian said. "I'll have to see if I can find a place for it."

"Can we go out this way?" Marie said.

"Of course," Frankie said. "Let me open the doors at the top of the stairs."

THEY LEFT HIM STANDING in the back yard, holding the envelope and waving it good-bye. They walked up the alley and into the street. "Would you like me to carry your bag?" Ian said.

"I wouldn't mind," she said, "it's awful heavy."

On Parle
Par Coeur

EVEN SO EARLY in the morning tourists filled the "Old Quebec" streets, but in the stone church there were only two, in t-shirts, sneakers, shorts and cameras. Her shirt said, "J'y suis, j'y reste." His said, "Le français, on le parle par coeur." She said, "For Christ's sake, Charlie, let's get out of here, we haven't got all day." He said, "Just a minute, darling, I think I see my Christmas card coming."

Graceful, Yvette walked up the side aisle. Frail, yet she moved with strength, like a straw in a rough broom, or a low note from a flute. A paisley dress, elastic at the waist, hung loose on her and hid her movements. She glided past the pews which were almost her height and shaped at the top like little church roofs. At the front, she knelt before a low tray of candles. A flash obliterated the dark of the church. She closed her eyes and thanked God for the death of her father.

Before Yvette's mother died, she called her to her room. "Yvette," she said.

"Yes, Mama."

"I am going to die."

"Yes, Mama."

"God looks after the dead, Yvette, but the living must get by on their own hook."

"Yes, Mama."

"Your father is old. He is older than me, but I am going to die first, anyway."

Yvette took her mother's hand. "Don't be in such a big hurry, Mama."

"You have the cow for milk. You have the chickens for eggs. You have a pig. You have a garden. You need money. Look after all these things and your father can do his work."

"Yes, Mama."

"It must be done before he comes home, or he will do it himself, or he will worry about it. He is too old to do it; and he is too old to worry about it."

"Yes, Mama."

"And if you can, you must keep walking him back home from work. He is strong but his heart will quit one day when he is walking up the hill. You wouldn't want him to be alone then."

"Yes, Mama."

"It'll keep you healthy, Yvette."

HER FATHER WORKED on the ferry, collecting tickets. Because he was old, they gave him the day shift which ended before the heavy after-work traffic; she could finish her chores by four and in a half hour run the three miles, arrive before the ferry docked after his last trip, and catch her breath before he stepped off.

It was uphill all the way back. Wolfe's men, on the other side, had trouble getting up even once; it's not surprising that they grumbled and complained. Yvette and her father did it every day, so they learned to save their breath. She took his lunch can in silence, and if the weather was warm his sweater, and in silence they walked, they climbed, up the ramp, past the railroad station, up the almost vertical wooden stairs; she knew if he had his heart attack on the stairs she could never hold him from flying to the pavement; up the steep path, through the gardens and driveways, across the road, through the fields.

About once a month, they had a conversation as she took his lunch box and sweater. It was either:

"Why not take a taxi, Papa?"

"No. The walks keep me alive."

Or:

"How did it go today, Papa?"

"The same. It's a funny thing. You spend your whole life going over and coming back every day. You never get off on the other side. You always come back."

But one day he did not come back. "Where is he, Gaston?"

"He got sick. They took him off the other side."

"Do you think he's all right?"

"Don't know," Gaston said.

She got on the ferry. On the other side she found him on his back. His eyes were wide, but seemed sightless. His fingers gripped the pavement. A line of people filed by moving toward the ferry. A tourist took a picture. The ambulance came. She got in with him.

She stayed at the hospital three months, going home to her chores every evening, and coming back in the morning. She trained him to move his arms and to smile. Then, to drink. Then to eat. Then she took him home, returning to the hospital in the evenings to work the night shift. In the day, she did her chores and read to her father. She went to the bookstore every day on her way to work and looked at the books, and every payday she bought a book. In the bookstore, she read the lives of the saints and when she finished a story, she would tell it to her father from memory. These always made him laugh. They lived happily like that for a year. Then she came home one morning, and he was there but he was not there. They lived like that for a year. She read to him, just in case, and watched for his smile, and she went to church every morning on her way to work and prayed that he would die. Finally he did.

She thanked God. And said to him: "Mais, Seigneur, maintenant, il m'en faut un autre."

"Un autre père?" God said, in mock puzzlement.

She pursed her lips, as if to scold a naughty but lovable child. "Non, non, silly. J'en ai fini avec des pères, il me faut un autre homme. J'ai besoin d'un chum."

"O.K.," God said. "That makes more sense."

WHEN SHE LEFT THE CHURCH, she crossed the street to the bookstore. She had no one to read to now but she kept her schedule. She read at the window, and as she read, she saw him go by. She leaned forward to look through the window up the street. She went to the door and leaned out, her finger in the book, but he had turned up the alley. She ran to the alley. There was no one there but artists, setting up pictures to sell to tourists. She returned to the store and stood again in the window and reread:

"St. John of the Road; a minor, legendary figure. As a youth, he grew bored with sin and retired to a hovel to become a solitary, reading what few books he had brought in his knapsack and working as a dishwasher for his food. When the veins in his calves became swollen and purple and sore, he began running the streets of the city. When he became tired, he would stop to rest and preach to the first person who came along."

Yvette looked up and saw him go by again. "It's him," she said.

"Pardon me," said the clerk. "May I help you?"

"No, thank you. I'm just browsing."

"You are not allowed to take books out on the street unless you pay for them."

He didn't come around again. But on the way to the bus stop, in the middle of the square, she found him, stretched out on the pavement, in front of a car with a bent fender, blood running from his nose. He had no shirt on his back and very little skin. "He ran in front of me," said the driver of the car.

"You didn't see him?" the policeman said.

"No, I didn't see him!" the man said and threw his arms in the air.

"How come you didn't see him?"

"I don't know. He came from nowhere."

"There's nothing here to jump from behind but wind and sunshine."

"I don't know. He was just there. Right in front of me." Suddenly, the injured man jumped up and ran. They watched him until he turned a corner.

When she got to work, he was there in the emergency room. "What's this one, George?" the doctor said.

"I don't know," the ambulance driver said. "Some kids found him on the Plains. He won't talk. No I.D. Nothing. He's a runner. No wallet, no tag, nothing." The doctor pulled off his sneakers and looked inside. "Anything there?"

"Eleven. He has big feet. What's your name?" he said. The eyes looked, but said nothing.

"In English, maybe. What is your name?" the doctor said in English. The eyes looked, but he said nothing. "Bang on the head, anyway," the doctor said. "Amnesia, maybe. Had a nosebleed but superficial, I think. Yvette, would you clean him up, dress the back of the wound there, his skin is in sheds, must be sore. Get him a head x-ray. I think he'll be O.K."

"O.K."

"See if you can find some place where someone can keep an eye on him. I'm supposed to go on vacation today, so let Dr. Marier know if he doesn't improve."

"Where will I put him?"

"God, I don't know. They've got them in the hallways upstairs. That's not bad enough, but half the staff is on strike. It's up to you. My vacation is half over and I'm still here."

"O.K."

"Don't forget the x-ray. Just in case. Get Marier to look at it. Soon as possible."

"D'accord." After the x-ray was checked out, she put him in the store room which she'd be in and out of all day.

THE EMERGENCY ROOM was crowded with holiday catastrophes plus a flood of people diverted from outpatient services because of the strike. She stole a moment to attend to him whenever she needed bandages or equipment from the store room. "T'es-tu fais mal?" The eyes looked at her but he said nothing. And she wondered how she was going to get him home. She knew he could walk, but would he? Would he sit up? Or get off the stretcher? And what about clothes? In shorts and sneakers and bandages, he would be too noticeable. In the locker room she found a shirt and a pair of pants. Although the runner would not respond to verbal commands he cooperated with physical persuasion. She put on the pants and shirt. She was deft at it after so many times dressing her father. "Lève-toi," she said. He didn't move but when she put her hand under his neck he sat up. She pulled his feet around and dropped them to the floor, pushed him to his feet by the neck and took his arm and away they went, to the bus stop, onto the bus, off, down the funicular, through Place St. Charles, onto the ferry, off, up the steep steps, up the gardens and driveways, across the road, up the field, home. She put him in her father's bed and gave him a pill with a glass of water.

Once he was asleep she took off his sneakers, the pants and shirt from the hospital, and his shorts. She put the hospital clothes in her large carpet bag to bring back to work. His sneakers and shorts she put in a laundry bag. Then she collected all her father's old clothes and took them and the laundry bag to the barn and buried them in the loft under the hay. Then she came back and her tiny fingers ran lightly all over his body, stopping here and there to savour the texture. "His hairs are beautiful," she thought, "but will he like me?" She turned him over on his belly and changed the dressing on his back. Scars were beginning to form already. She stood and looked him over. What a cute bum, she thought, and gave each cheek a little slap and watched it shiver. "He will like me," she thought, "probably." She covered him with a sheet.

After her chores were done, he was still asleep. She went to bed and dozed until she heard him. When she got to his room, he was wrapped in the sheet, looking in the closet. She beckoned to him. "Come," she said, and led him to the bathroom. "In there." He went in and she shut the door behind him and pursed her lips and raised her eyes, and went to his bedroom and sat on his bed and waited. He was a long time and when he did come back, she had to get off the bed and back up to the window before he would en-ter the room. Then he got into bed, still wrapped in the sheet, with his knees up, and his ankles in the grip of his hands. She came back then and sat on the edge of the bed, slowly, as you might try to get close to a rabbit.

"Comment tu t'appelles?" He looked at her and tried to smile, but squinted instead like someone surprised by a mouthful of warm water. "What's your name?" she said again. He looked at the door. "You have forgotten how to talk," she said. "You will have to learn all over again. I will teach you. Do you understand...never mind. It's simple enough to learn when you have lots of time. But we won't start 'til tomorrow. Tonight relax." She tried to take his feet in her hands and pull his legs out straight, but he wouldn't let them go. Her hands went under the sheet to pry his fingers from his ankles but his hands were too strong. So she got up on the bed behind him and massaged his neck and head and shoulders until he gave in and stretched out on his side. She pushed him over on his belly and soothed him with her fingers until he was asleep. She woke ahead of him in the morning and woke him up and gave him a vitamin and a pill crushed in a glass of milk. He stayed asleep then until she was back from work and had the chores done. She had the next two days off.

"Wine," her father used to say, so she started off with two large glasses of dusky burgundy with a dusky taste that clung to the hairs of the tongue like a bit of cloth, served on a tray, placed between them on a bed-table she had borrowed from the hospital when her father was sick.

"Did you have a nice day?" she asked and when he didn't answer, she picked up the newspaper from the foot of the bed and read to him. "There will be a congruence of events and a stranger will stand at a crossroads. That's my horoscope, for today," she said. "What's your birthday?" He took a sip of burgundy. "I have a feeling it's today," she said. "Listen to this. 'The slate is wiped clean. A new beginning is possible. Leap before you look.' Isn't that interesting?" she said, and took the glasses and left the room. With the porterhouse steak, and the mushrooms picked from the pasture and sautéed in butter, and the celery sticks filled with homemade cheese, and the potatoes baked, split, and filled with sour cream, and peas, picked from the garden and served raw, she gave another burgundy.

When his plate was empty and his last sip of wine sipped, she asked, "More?" and he understood, and nodded yes. "Ah yes, I know," she said, "a runner's food goes first to his feet, and then he eats for his belly. I have more. And I'll open more wine."

After he had finished again, she took away the dishes and came back with the glasses refilled. She wheeled away the bed table and sat at the foot of the bed, cross-legged. "Here's to learning to speak," she raised her glass. He raised his, but said nothing. "My name is Yvette." He looked at her and opened his mouth, but said nothing. She pulled out a notebook and pen from her pocket and wrote, "Yvette," and handed it to him.

"Yvette," he said.

"Yvette," she said and poked herself between her breasts.

"Yvette."

"Yvette," he said, and nodded.

"And you," she said, and leaned forward and touched his chest. He shook his head back and forth. "Abraham is what I will call you," she said. "Abraham Runner," she reached and touched him. "Yvette," she said and pointed.

"Yvette," he agreed.

"Abraham," she pointed.

"Abraham," he pointed to himself.

"Formidable," she said. "My name is Yvette," she said. Then she wrote it and gave it to him, and repeated, "My name is Yvette."

"My name is Yvette," he said.

"Mais no," she said. "My name is Yvette."

"Yvette," he agreed.

She passed him another note. "My name is Abraham," it said. She opened her palm to him, an invitation to speak.

"My name is Abraham," he said.

"D'accord," she said. "O.K. My name is Yvette." And she opened her palm.

"My name is Abraham," he said.

"Your name is Abraham," she said. And she passed him a note.

"Your name is Yvette," he read and pointed.

"Wow," she said. "That's it. We're on the way. I am a woman," she said, and covered her breasts with her hands.

"A woman."

"A woman," he agreed. She passed him a note and said, "You are a man," she said and pointed between his legs.

"I am a man," he read, and pointed between his legs. And he smiled, finally.

"My name is Yvette," she said.

"My name is Abraham," he said.

"I am a woman," she said.

"I am a man," he said. Then smiled. They relaxed. They laughed and finished their glasses. Yvette went out to the kitchen and came back with their glasses refilled, on a wooden tray which had a fish carved into it, one glass of burgundy at the head and one at the tail, and in between them a chocolate cake with a burning candle in the center. She put it on the middle of the bed and resumed her cross-legged position at the foot. "Blow it out," she said, and pointed to the candle between them and made blowing motions with her mouth. He leaned over the cake and blew out the candle and they watched as a thread of smoke rose toward the ceiling. She got up, as if pulled by the smoke and stood on the bed and raised her glass. "Here's to Abraham," she said, but her knees buckled and landed in the cake and the glass of wine toppled from her hand and landed upside down on Abraham's head, and ran down his face and splashed burgundy stains over the white sheet. "My God, my God!" she said. "What have I done? My cake is ruined, my legs are soaked, my sheets are splattered, my bed is a mess, I should be angry, I should be crying, but I'm happy, and I can't help laughing."

ONCE THE SPEAKING LESSONS were well under way and progress was steady and success certain, she brought him her father's clothes. She taught him how to milk the cow, and he began to do the chores while she was at work. Each day as she climbed to her home she felt apprehension like fluid swelling her glands until she caught sight of him standing in the orchard, or waving to her from the barn, or toasting her with a glass of water through the kitchen window panes.

One day when she came home, he was standing in the garden with his two hands and his chin on the handle of the hoe. She had to throw a rock onto the steel roof of the barn to get his attention. He sent her a long slow wave. Inside, in the bedroom on the desk where he worked, she found a piece of writing paper. The word Halifax was written on it. It was a word she knew. She yelled to him from the window. "Did you milk the cow?" "No. Not yet." "I'll do it," she yelled. "We can eat later." She went to the barn, and sat on the little three-legged stool, and put her head against the warm belly of the cow and pulled on the teats and poured milk and tears into the pail. After that her apprehension would not subside. She examined his work every day. She could make out very few words, but she counted the pages. He surprised her at it one day. He smiled. "Did you find it interesting?" he said.

"Are you here," she said, "with me? Or are you gone?"

"Je t'aime," he said. She smiled. But she noticed for the first time that he was looking at her through holes in the air.

CONTINUED ON NEXT PAGE